ROSE WULF

Evernight Publishing

www.evernightpublishing.com

Copyright© 2016

Rose Wulf

Editor: Audrey Bobak

Cover Artist: Jay Aheer

ISBN: 978-1-77233-871-3

ALL RIGHTS RESERVED

ROSE WULF

DEDICATION

To Jim & Donna Conroy and David "Uncle Homey" & Margie Parry,
for the lifetime of laughs and memories I've collected every summer.

For the love of good friends who are like family.

Donna, as requested, I give you a character named Starlette.

Aunt Margie, I may have borrowed a joke or two!

ROSE WULF

BLACK DAWN

Dark Light, 1

Rose Wulf

Copyright © 2016

Prologue

Dark, powerful forces live in the shadows. Forces that would have taken over everything long ago if not for the light that keeps the shadows at bay. This is a war that has been raging since the dawn of man and will likely continue until the end. But, for most of that time, it has been waged in silence.

Until recently.

A powerful demon, rumored to be the son of Satan himself, devised a new plan to gain ground against the arrogant angels. And, as a result, the very real existence of demons was revealed to the more influential, more connected humans. All it took was one lopsided deal for word to spread, and with every curious mind soon followed a lost soul. Another soul for Satan's army. A few real, and rather effective, spells leaked to that glorious invention the humans called 'internet', and in no time the tide had turned.

Corrupt, selfish, desperate humans sold their souls in droves. And every now and then a new piece of text, connected to dark demonic magic, would make its way into the hands of mankind. Soon humans weren't just summoning under a full moon at a crossroads, but in the comfort of their living room. Not just to exact a heartfelt vengeance, but to be sure they passed their final exams.

The angels began to lose ground. Their pure, naïve souls that they so valiantly defended were leaping of their own free will into the clutches of Hell. They had to take action, to go on the offensive in a way they hadn't considered for eons. A leader was chosen—a most powerful angel with a new perspective and an ancient respect. Her name was Isabella, and she, in turn, built an army. She called for the training of another, not wanting to be caught unawares should her first army fall.

And she sent them into battle.

The angels and the demons have been fighting for control of the Earth from the beginning. They fight as though there is a chance one can truly win, standing on their respective sides and raising their swords to the skies with eager battle cries.

Neither ever considered that their hatred of each other was something less than true…

Chapter One

Then

Isolde Duchane sat between two silent men, at her father's insistence, and watched as her mother was buried in an elaborate box. Her black dress was itchy and she hated it, but she understood black was the color to be worn at funerals. She also understood it was okay for her to cry—that was her mother in the box. It was her mother everyone behind her had come to say goodbye to. And it was the loss of her mother that was responsible for her father's unusual behavior. He'd dropped to his knees in front of the hole, mindless of the chill in the wind or the dirt flying in his face. And though she couldn't see his face, she knew he was crying.

Izzy sniffled and wiped at her cheeks with the back of her hand, smearing tears and snot across the lacey glove. She didn't care. She would never wear any part of this outfit again.

Someone's hand reached forward and gave her shoulder a squeeze. "Be strong, Izzy," the person said. She knew without looking that it was her friend's mother, because of course her friend had come. She just wished she could be sitting with them, instead of isolated between two security guards.

Her mother would never have forced her to sit with security at a time like this.

Mommy... She'd be the only girl in her class with a parent in the ground now. Sure, by middle school lots of her classmates had parents who'd separated. Some had remarried, some were seeing people but not living with them. But so far as Izzy knew they were all alive somewhere. Because eleven year olds weren't supposed to have to visit a grave to visit their moms and dads.

****

Izzy jerked awake late one night by a loud *boom* that was immediately followed by the shaking of her bedroom. The glowing display on her clock read one-thirteen and her stomach clenched immediately in fear. *Daddy!*

She threw aside her blankets and ran for the door, hoping the loud noise had come from the television. But that hope vanished when she ran into a veritable wall of smoke so thick and acrid she nearly threw up. Whatever that smell was, it was disgusting. And it was coming from downstairs.

Izzy made it down the rounded staircase in record time, unsurprised to see security gathering in the main room. "Where's my dad?" she cried, running up to Roland. He was their head of night security. If anyone knew what was going on, it was him.

"Isolde, just stay with me," Roland replied, his eyes squinted from the smoke still filling the room.

The smoke alarm finally went off when Izzy's attention landed on the open door to her father's study. Even through the haze she could tell the smoke, and whatever had caused it, was coming from there. "Daddy!"

She felt a larger hand brush her arm, as if intending to hold her back, but she threw her weight to the side as she sprinted forward and slipped easily through the group. They were too scattered to stop her, and that meant they couldn't tell her anything, either. But if her father were still up—and he probably was—he'd be in that room.

Please, not Daddy, too! "Daddy!" she called again, catching herself against the doorframe and coughing into her hand. "*Daddy!*"

All at once the smoke vanished, like it had been sucked right out of the air by an invisible vacuum. Izzy's brown eyes went wide as she saw her father, standing with a kerchief over his mouth and nose, backed up against his desk. The desk had been pushed against the far wall. In fact, Izzy slowly realized, the entire office was a mess. She figured that was all because of the other man, the unfamiliar, dark figure standing in the exact center of the room with his back to her.

He was *really* tall, with long hair that had to be the blackest black she'd ever seen, and shoulders so broad she could probably sit her whole butt on just one of them. She'd never seen anyone like him, not even when her father had taken her with him to his big business meetings in Europe. He looked strong, and with his fists clenched the way they were, Izzy could easily imagine being frightened of him. From her angle, in fact, her father looked somewhat afraid.

"Isolde, I said to stay back!" Roland snapped as he caught up to her and his free hand landed on Izzy's shoulder, startling her enough to make her jump and squeak.

The stranger in her father's office spun in place, fists clenching tighter, and leveled on Roland a glare darker than his pitch-black hair. For a moment the hand on her shoulder tightened, before falling away altogether as the guard took a cautious step backward. But Izzy barely noticed. She was captivated by the stranger's face. His glare was focused so intently on Roland it was like he didn't see her at all, and despite the dark expression he wore, Izzy found herself fascinated.

Somehow, she knew immediately what this stranger was. He was a demon. But what was a demon doing in her father's office? She'd always heard demons were violent, dangerous, and that she should run far and fast if she ever caught sight of one. But this one didn't scare her at all, and for him to have appeared in her father's office like he had had to mean her father had *summoned* him. Didn't it?

"Izzy, sweetheart," her father called on cue, his voice surprisingly calm. The demon's expression faded to nearly neutral, though Izzy noticed he kept his focus on the guard. He was like a statue. Or a hunting dog. "It's okay," her father continued, reaching out carefully. Encouragingly. "Come here, please."

"Sir?" Roland questioned.

The demon's eyes narrowed.

"Stand down," Izzy's father instructed. "Everything's under control."

Izzy released a breath, her father's calm voice assuring her that her instincts were right. She sprinted forward, not caring about her proximity to the stranger, and wrapped her arms around her father's waist. "I was scared, Daddy!" she cried. "I thought—"

"Shh," her father interrupted gently. "I'm sorry to scare you," he said. "I just had to do this at night, you understand." He pried her from him, stroked her frizzy, more-orange-than-red hair, and smiled. "Izzy, I want to introduce you to someone."

Her eyes stung as her gaze followed her father's arm as he gestured toward the stranger-demon, who had turned around once more and was watching them. His expression was entirely neutral now, and his fists had relaxed at his sides.

"Izzy," Gerald Duchane began, an odd mix of pride and reluctance in his voice, "this demon is called Darr. He will be protecting you from now on."

Izzy's eyes widened and she looked back up at her father. "Why? I don't need a bodyguard!" Nor was this even the first time she'd had to tell him that. Since her mother's death months earlier he'd been obsessed over two things, one of which was making sure she was overly protected at every single turn. Still, he'd never taken it *this* far.

Gerald dropped a hand to her head with a sad, patient smile. "After what happened to your mother … I just want to know that you're safe. It's a dangerous world we live in, honey, and I won't be able to be around all the time."

Scrunching up her face, Izzy glanced back at Darr and found that, this time, he was staring straight at her. Unblinking. And as intimidating as his stare was, she wasn't afraid. She certainly didn't need a bodyguard, but how many kids at school could say they had a *demon* protecting them? "Hi," she said with a small, shy smile. "I'm Izzy."

"Give him your hand, Izzy," Gerald instructed. "He needs a pure source of your scent, in case you ever get lost."

Izzy lifted her attention back to her father. He was making less sense with each word. But before she could say anything strong, warm, rough fingers had wrapped around her wrist and lifted her arm for her. By the time she looked forward again Darr, who had knelt in order to accommodate their difference in height, had pressed his nose almost completely against the heel of her palm. All she could do was watch, eyes wide, as Darr inhaled deeply. Once, twice, three times. Then he lowered her wrist until he was holding her hand in a loose, casual handshake and he met her gaze again.

"Good evening, Izzy," Darr said. His voice was as strong and deep as he was tall. She'd never heard one like it.

Smiling, and not knowing what else to say, Izzy repeated, "Hi."

****

Darr couldn't believe his luck. One minute he was running for his life from some very pissed off slavers and the next thing he knew, a summoning portal of sorts popped up right in front of him. It didn't take an idiot to know wherever that portal landed was a damned sight better than where he was, so he'd plowed right through and breathed a sigh of relief when it closed behind him.

He never would have guessed the portal would land him in front of some rich, undoubtedly moronic human. A human who'd still been stumbling over his tongue when another, younger human burst into the room.

"Daddy!" she'd cried. And that was all it took. That was all Darr needed to hear or see to know that the little girl was the key—not just to his answers, but to his freedom.

Still, he hadn't wanted to let his decision show until he got some of those answers. Answers Gerald Duchane was more than willing to provide. And it turned out the man thought he'd deliberately summoned him. Not only that, but he believed he'd bound Darr using a Life Bind. Which was rich, because from what Darr could tell, Duchane was lucky he'd even opened a portal into Hell at all. The man had *no* affinity for spells.

Fortunately, Duchane's intent was Darr's perfect solution. If he played along and pretended to be bound to the girl, Isolde Duchane, then he would be free of his abusers for a good eighty or ninety years. They'd have stopped looking for him *long* before that, and then it would be safe to return home.

"You know how these Life Binds work, right?" Duchane asked.

Darr narrowed his eyes. "I do." *Better than you.*

Duchane bobbed his head. "Good, good. Then you start immediately. I want *nothing* to hurt my daughter, you understand? Not ever."

"I understand," Darr assured him easily. "I'll take her to bed."

Duchane looked around the space and sighed. "Thank you. I'd best get this mess cleaned up." He paused just long enough for Darr to turn and start toward the door before calling, "Oh, and come morning I expect you to look presentable. Izzy's the only heir to the Duchane name. She's expected to keep a certain class of company."

Darr only nodded sharply before leaving the man alone in the room. *Presentable, huh?* He happened to think he looked perfectly fine, but humans obviously had another standard. So he studied the guards—all of whom were giving him skeptical, frightened looks—as he and the girl passed. And he noticed what they all had in common. Short hair and identical black suits. *Fucking cliché.*

But he'd do what he had to for now.

Izzy showed him the way to her room and allowed him to tuck her in, but when he turned back after checking to be sure her window was secured, she was sitting up again.

"Sleep," he instructed.

She ignored him. "Why does Daddy think I need a demon?"

Darr bit back his sigh. "You'll have to ask him. He didn't enlighten me."

Izzy scrunched her lips in a pout and looked at a picture on her nightstand. The woman in the photograph had smoothed, red hair and faded, green eyes. She looked a lot like he imagined Izzy would when she reached adulthood. "Is it because of what happened to Mommy?"

At this he frowned. Instinct insisted the simple answer was 'yes', but he would prefer to know what he was agreeing to first. "What happened to Mommy?"

Eyes downcast and voice soft, Izzy replied, "She died. I don't think Daddy knows I know, but she was killed. And I'm pretty sure no one knows who did it."

So that's it. Darr moved forward until he had rested another hand on her shoulder. "That's probably why I'm here now," he agreed. "But enough about that. You need to sleep."

Izzy obediently laid back down and rolled onto her side, facing him. "Will you be here when I wake up?"

Darr nodded. "Yes."

Chapter Two

Now

The first ten or fifteen years were easy once he learned what was normal and what wasn't in Izzy's world. He just stood back for the most part and judged her father's declining sanity. Twice in the past twenty-one years Izzy—or her father, and her through him—had been targeted by demons. Both times due to her father's idiotic, dangerous business practices. A handful of times other non-demonic, but still serious, threats had popped up. And Darr had handled them all with equal efficiency.

In all honesty, though, she'd never really needed a full-time demonic bodyguard.

And for the first decade and a half he'd been fairly bored with the work. Until one day he'd woken up and realized that little Izzy Duchane had matured sometime while he wasn't paying attention.

She still preferred to go by Izzy, her orange-red hair was still a mess when she woke up every morning, and she was still too trusting of strangers. But aside from the additional fact that she was, of course, still *human*, nothing else remained of the child he'd met just over two decades earlier. Izzy was thirty-two years old, full-bodied, confident, assertive, and a daily temptation.

Most of the time that temptation came in the form of lust. Today, it seemed, the bigger temptation was not to cripple her. Or, rather, not to physically restrain her. The woman was pushing his last nerve.

"—*Really* not that big a deal," Izzy continued, unaware of the fact that he'd tuned out her entire argument. "It's *one* weekend."

Darr leaned back against the counter, schooling his face into neutral as she cocked a hip as if her body language could make her point for her. *Well, it does make a point ... but not the one she means.* "I don't know why you're asking my permission," he replied aloud. Resting his palms over the cool granite surface behind him he added, "You can go wherever you want."

Izzy heaved a dramatic sigh. "Yes," she acknowledged, "but this time I need to go *without* you. I can't really be bringing my demon bodyguard with me to my best friend's bachelorette party."

Restraining his scowl for the moment, Darr said, "I could lie if you want."

"No, I don't want that," Izzy returned immediately before stalking up to him so as to stick her finger in his chest. "I want you to *agree* to do this my way."

How many times were they going to have a variation of this argument? It probably wasn't a good idea to keep count.

"Sorry. Not happening."

Izzy's brown eyes lit with frustration and she stepped back, hands on hips. "Come *on*, Darr! How dangerous could it really be? I know how to defend myself!"

"If I could see the future, I'd tell you," he said. "But since that's not in my repertoire, I'm going with you. Because *once* is all it takes."

Her mouth opened with obvious intent to continue the argument, but she paused and something else flickered in her brown gaze. A beat later her breath rushed out in a sigh of defeat and she turned, waving absently as she said, "Fine, I give up. You can come. But you have to be as *invisible* as *possible*, okay? Britt asked me not to bring you."

That was because Britt was both terrified and attracted to him at the same time. And seeing as how it was her bachelorette party Izzy was attending over the weekend, Darr figured she probably didn't want to spend it fighting an unrequited ache for another man. But he couldn't tell Izzy that much because the knowledge would just make her uncomfortable. All Izzy knew was that her friend didn't like being near him.

"Don't worry," Darr offered as he trailed after her. "I don't intend on making small talk."

To this comment Izzy barked out a laugh and turned a teasing grin to him. "Actually, I would *pay* to see that. Darr-the-dangerous making small talk!"

He let the scowl slip through this time. She knew he hated that nickname.

Izzy laughed again and brushed him off. "I'm going to be upstairs packing. You don't have to follow if you don't want to, it's not like I'll be out of range."

Darr inclined his head and took a seat on her sofa. He generally tried to let her have her privacy in her bedroom now that she'd reached maturity. 'Generally' being the operative word. She still sometimes had nightmares about the harder times from her childhood, like her mother's murder and the one time another demon had managed to lay hands on her. When she had nightmares, she preferred him to stay, to stand guard so that she knew she was safe.

Those were the nights he stood guard *inside* her room.
****

"I thought I asked you not to bring him!" Britt hissed as soon as the women were alone in their cabin. The three of them—Izzy, bride-to-be Britt, and mutual friend Letty—were sharing the largest lakeside cabin of the small resort. Britt's future sister-in-law and her close friend were sharing the other, smaller cabin next door. Darr was currently walking the property, judging its

19

safety and likely wondering why he'd argued to come at all.

Izzy sighed and sat on the foot of her chosen bed. "Come on, Britt, when do I go anywhere without him? He's supposed to protect me and he can't exactly do his job if I'm two hours away." By car. Which he would probably not bother with, since he was a demon and they had much faster ways to travel. Even after all these years she still didn't understand how that worked, but work it did.

Britt pursed her lips and looked away. "I told you, he creeps me out. I don't want to be having nightmares this weekend."

"I don't see the big deal," Letty interrupted, settling on the foot of her own bed. With a teasing grin she added, "He's deliciously sexy. Hell, I'd show him my address if he let me."

Both Izzy and Britt looked at her in confused silence.

Finally Izzy repeated, "Show him your address?" Letty had said it like a sexual innuendo, but how in the world did that count as a sexual thing?

Shrugging, Letty replied, "It's something my aunt said. When I asked her about it once she explained it as 'when a man looks at you between your legs'."

"Oh my God," Britt exclaimed, turning her back as if to ward off the thought.

Izzy burst out laughing and collapsed on her mattress. "Wow, Letty, that's a new one!" Because it was easier to focus on how amusingly silly that comment was than to think about Darr and Letty—or Darr and anyone—in an intimate way. She imagined there *had* to be some nights Darr snuck off while she slept and hooked up with someone somewhere, because no way could a man as sexy as him go over twenty years without any action. But she didn't really like to *think* about it. Those thoughts only brought up pointless jealousy and useless pining or self-pity.

"Could we please talk about something else?" Britt insisted, acting as though her face wasn't flushed.

Letty's grin was apparent in her voice. "Oh, fine, fine. It's more important that we talk about your sex life, anyway. How are you and Jude? Compatible in the sack, I hope."

Izzy did her best to contain herself as she pushed to a sitting position and watched her best friend turn redder.

Britt released an indignant scoff. "Is sex all you can think about today?"

"Apparently," Letty replied. With a shrug she added, "In my defense, I haven't gotten any in *months*. Makes me want to try dating again."

Izzy stood and crossed the space to sit beside Letty, looping an arm around her shoulder. "Silver lining, Letty. At least you've had action in the past few years." At the look of horror both women replied with, Izzy offered a helpless gesture. "Downside of a studious demon bodyguard. He never sleeps."

Letty laughed, exclaiming, "I'm telling you, Izzy, I could give you tips on what to do about that."

Britt spoke up practically before Letty was done. "Why do you keep turning the conversation back to that guy? I thought I said I didn't want to be thinking about him."

Izzy sobered and looked away, realizing she'd done it again. Britt had pointed it out to her several times over the years and it never stuck. Apparently she had a bad habit of rounding all conversations back to Darr. *But how can't I?* He was the most reliable, stable, and longest-lasting aspect of her life.

She'd had a mother for a mere eleven years. Sometime during her teens her father had distanced himself from her, or she from him maybe. They'd had their share of disputes as she'd grown. She'd had a few boyfriends, some good friends—all of whom were gone now. Britt was the next in line behind Darr in many ways, as they'd met in high school, but Darr was hands down her rock. The single being she most trusted and relied on. So of course he was always on her mind.

Or it could be because I'm— Nope. Not going there this time. Really, there was no sense in thinking *that*.

"Sorry, Britt." She paused, stood, and said, "It's early enough, what say we throw on those new swimsuits and go sunning?"

Britt broke out in a smile and gave her a short hug. "I knew I loved you," she joked before moving to her discarded suitcase. Behind them Letty made a squeal of delight and sprang to her feet as well.

Izzy moved to her suitcase as well and extracted the new bikini Britt had talked her into purchasing. She hadn't worn something so provocative since her mid-twenties, but Britt assured her she could pull it off. So when it was her turn in the spacious bathroom, she took her time examining her figure in the large window. She wasn't indecent, thank goodness, but she was definitely flaunting her C-cups. And she was so immensely glad Darr had always been insistent on her staying in good shape. If she had any more of a belly she'd be too embarrassed to leave the cabin. But the emerald-green bikini was very flattering against her paler skin and bright hair.

She had the uncharacteristic urge to take a bathroom selfie and was suddenly glad she hadn't brought her cell in with her.

Letty whistled when Izzy stepped out. "Isolde Duchane, I haven't seen you in a bikini this good since college. I approve."

Izzy cringed at the use of her proper name. Really, of all people to prefer a nickname, *Starlette* should have understood.

"I told you you could rock that," Britt declared with a proud grin and a hand on her hip. "Are we all ready, ladies?"
****

Fuck.

Maybe he should have given in this time and let Izzy come to this resort without him. He hadn't actually seen the suit she'd picked up at the mall with Britt the week before. And that was a good thing. Unfortunately, now that he had seen her, he couldn't look away.

Izzy walked ahead of him, beside Britt, with a towel over her shoulder and her hair up in a frizzy ponytail. Flip flops on her feet, sunglasses over her eyes, and her arm looped through Britt's, she looked like a woman without a care. He ought to have just taken pride in that and moved on, but damn it all his eyes were practically glued to that ass. Perfectly round and oh-so-barely covered by the smooth, simple, emerald-colored fabric. He could envision holding that ass in his hands, preferably without the swimsuit at all—and that was as far as he'd allow that fantasy to go.

He never expected he'd feel this way about the human he'd willingly tied himself to. At most he'd anticipated spending the first few years after her death feeling confused and maybe sad. But now… He didn't like to think about it at all.

"—Can't bodysurf on a lake!" Britt exclaimed with a laugh as Darr tuned back in.

Letty laughed and clapped Britt's shoulder. "You can if the boats are going fast enough!"

The women slowed, looking for a good spot to spread out their towels, and Darr slowed obligingly. He had, after all, promised to be as inconspicuous as he could. It was simply hard to be inconspicuous when he was a 6'6" 'hard ass' demon, as Izzy often said. They chose a spot, Izzy considerately taking the spot closest to the shade line, and Darr rested a shoulder against a tree trunk. They'd be sunbathing and swimming for a couple of hours, probably. It was fortunate they'd chosen a smaller resort. Darr had only discovered two other pairs occupying the other cabins. A couple in their sixties and a father and son who'd been leaving to fish the lake.

His attention shifted as he noticed the other half of the bachelorette party approach. Britt's future sister-in-law, Ainsley McManus, and Britt's cousin who happened to also be Ainsley's good friend. He forgot the cousin's name. The cousin was the only one not wearing a revealing bikini, but he barely registered the needless detail. They may as well all have been wearing baggy sweats for all he cared.

"How many demons get to spend their days watching a bunch of human women flaunt bodies like that?"

Darr slid his gaze to the side to study the newcomer. It was Zahk, one of his few friends. They'd met centuries earlier before Zahk had been sold off to a master who'd shortly died and thereby given Zahk his freedom. They'd reconnected sometime in the past decade quite by accident, but Izzy had encouraged their friendship. And so long as Zahk continued to respect that his priority was Izzy's safety, Darr was happy to spend time with his friend.

"More than we know, probably," Darr finally replied. "What brings you out here?"

Zahk moved to lean against an opposite tree so he could face Darr and still see the women. "Come on, why can't a guy check in on his friends from time to time? You're terrible about answering my calls."

"You know I can't leave Izzy alone."

With a dramatic eye roll Zahk said, "You could return a voicemail."

Darr cringed and looked back to his friend. "Sorry," he offered. "I lost my phone a couple weeks back. Haven't bothered to replace it yet."

Zahk arched a dark brow at him. "I never took you for lazy."

Izzy's shriek tore Darr's attention and he nearly lurched forward before he realized what had happened. One of her friends had snuck up behind her and dunked her in the lake unceremoniously. She was already laughing and splashing them back.

Zahk chuckled, the sound dark and echoing. "You know, for one of the scariest bastards I've ever met, you're such a puppy with that one." He made a whipping sound for effect in case Darr had missed the point— which he had not.

Relaxing against the tree, Darr reflexively replied, "Her life is tied to mine, remember? She dies, I die, that sort of thing."

To this Zahk gave him a somber, long stare. There was disbelief in his eyes. "Yeah," he said. "About that… Word on the street is Old Duchane's not all that good with spells. I mean, there was that whole succubus thing last year."

Darr pinched the bridge of his nose. Yeah, *that* had been a nightmare. Idiot man had needed a date for a professional shindig and thought he'd coerce a pretty demon into putting on a sexy act. And boy had she. If Izzy hadn't stopped by with the rental suit he'd needed, the man would probably be dead.

And Darr's secret would be blown out of the water.

"For one thing," Zahk continued, "how come you didn't let it happen? You'd be free, you know. I mean, *really* free."

"I'm fine here," Darr insisted. "I already have the freedom I craved." And that, at least, was entirely true. He really had no desire to leave Izzy at this point, and any time spent dwelling on that reality disturbed him.

"This isn't freedom," Zahk argued. "This is just another breed of slavery. You're trapped in this deal so long as Old Duchane lives." He pushed off the tree and moved to clap his hand on Darr's shoulder. "Darr, buddy to buddy here, let me kill him for you. You're not bound to protect him and Izzy doesn't have to know until she's back in civilization."

Glaring, Darr spun to face his friend. "No. You won't lay a finger in any way on Duchane, is that clear?"

Zahk stepped back, brown eyes wide. "What, do you *care* about that drunk?"

It was hard not to scoff at the idea. Quite frankly he all but detested the moron. But no matter her qualms with her father, Izzy still loved him. Most days. And he had no intention of allowing her to feel the pain of that kind of loss—again. "No," he said. "But I was told to protect Izzy from *everything*. Including avoidable emotional pain." It was a stretch, but a truthful one.

"I can't imagine Old Duchane knew how to be so specific." Sighing, he turned toward the parking lot. "I'm not in the mood for this now. Have fun sporting that hard-on you won't do anything about." And then the shadows rose up, seeming to tug him into the ground as he vanished.

Darr ground his teeth and turned his attention back to Izzy. She didn't seem to have noticed his brief companion and he was glad. But what Zahk had said rang in his ears and a weight settled in his gut. Was he planning something? Had the suggestion actually been a subtle warning?

****

"*Please* tell me where you found that place, Ainsley," Britt pleaded as the women let themselves into the larger cabin after dinner. "That meal was delicious."

"It was just a little thing called Google," Ainsley said with a laugh.

"Now that we're all fed and we all have some alcohol in our systems," Letty said, "who's ready for a game? I brought all the dirty ones!"

Letty's hand was on the suitcase supposedly filled with naughty games when Izzy felt a tell-tale tingle trickle over her skin. She lifted her eyes to the darkest corner of the cabin—the corner beside her chosen bed, of course—just as Darr stepped into view.

"Izzy," he called in his deep, rough timbre.

Ainsley and Britt's cousin both cried out in surprise and even Britt and Letty jumped.

"Is that—?" Ainsley whispered with a glance toward Britt.

"Izzy!" Britt cried, a mixture of fright and frustration in her voice. She really did hate being around him.

Izzy apologized and waved her hand in their direction to pacify them as she moved up to her bodyguard. "What is it?" She knew for a fact he'd have continued hiding in shadowy corners silently if there wasn't something important on his mind.

"Not here," he said quietly, his voice sending delightful shivers down her spine. He reached out without another word, and wrapped a single arm around her waist before stepping back with her into the shadows. Izzy closed her eyes to minimize the disorientation as he transported them to a private location, her hands twisted in his tight, black shirt.

A moment later the sensation of movement faded and his grip loosened, though he made no move to step back until she released his shirt.

Lifting her gaze to his ashen one, Izzy repeated her earlier question. "What is it, Darr? Is something wrong?" She thought she'd seen Zahk with him earlier, but she thought nothing of it—Zahk was known to show up randomly from time to time. Had it not been a pleasant visit? Or was this something else?

Darr's expression was somber. "I'm worried there will be an attempt on your father's life tonight."

Sucking in a breath, Izzy gasped, "*What*? Why?"

"Zahk was here earlier," Darr replied. "It was something he said. I think he was trying to warn me."

Pressing a hand over her heart, Izzy stepped into Darr and rested her head on his chest. *Dad...* It wouldn't be the first time he'd angered someone—human or demon—to the point where his life was threatened. The first time he'd crossed that line, her mother had paid the ultimate price, and when he hadn't learned from that lesson, Izzy eventually came to the conclusion that she needed to distance herself from him. But she still loved him.

Arm coming around her again, this time in an embrace, Darr rumbled a soft question. "What do you want me to do, Izzy?"

Tears stinging her eyes, Izzy swallowed them back and inhaled a deep lungful of his scent. Crisp like mountain air, with just a hint of molasses. "I know you don't like going," she acknowledged, "but please don't let him die. Not like that."

Darr was silent for a long minute, undoubtedly debating her request with his situation. But finally his hold tightened as he embraced her and his lips came to the side of her ear. "Stay inside, stay safe, and call for me if anything happens. I'll be back before morning."

Her heart warmed at the intimate way he held her and the tender tone in his voice. He might be a demon, but as far as she was concerned he was really her guardian angel. *Or a knight in shining armor, maybe?* "Thank you," she whispered.

He loosened his hold, nodding when their eyes met, and took her hand in his. The next thing she knew her stomach was bottoming out and her feet were standing once again on an old wooden floor in a dark corner. But Darr wasn't with her.

Releasing a breath, Izzy wiped her palms on the sides of her jeans and turned to look for her friends just as Letty spoke up.

"Is … everything okay?"

"Izzy?" Britt asked, concern echoing in her voice. Despite her dislike of Darr, she still understood his purpose in Izzy's life. And Izzy appreciated it.

But she didn't want to dampen the night with Darr's suspicions when he would certainly foil this latest attempt on her father's life. So she smiled and moved more properly into the room. "Sorry. Everything's … fine. There's just a situation he has to deal with, so you guys are officially responsible for my well-being." The last was said teasingly. Aside from Darr, Izzy herself was the only one responsible for her well-being and she knew it.

Chapter Three

Not particularly wanting to engage in any sort of conversation with Gerald Duchane, Darr opted to keep to the shadows and keep himself hidden.

The man in question was watching accident videos on YouTube and alternating between Facebook messages—one for business and one with a woman who wouldn't likely ever agree to meet him. Darr didn't feel like prying deeper into it. Duchane's standard security team was all in place, the system armed and running. As usual Duchane's warding was wrong, leaving his home exposed to preternatural forces like Darr himself. Unfortunately, just fixing the warding wouldn't assure no demons slipped in. All it would take was an outdoor possession and a burst of dark energy.

Duchane's phone rang and the man paused his video to put the smaller device to his ear. "Yes?"

Darr expanded his senses to hear the other side of the conversation, despite knowing he'd then have to smell the man who drank too much. As he'd expected, alcohol and cigar smoke assaulted his nose immediately. But it couldn't be helped.

"Sir," a controlled male voice Darr didn't recognize said. "There's a woman here for you."

"Ah, excellent," Duchane declared, promptly shutting the lid of his laptop. Not a word to either message recipient. "Let her in, please. And offer to park her car around back for her. She'll be here a while."

Darr shuddered at the implications. This explained why the stench in the room was several hours old. Duchane was expecting company. Company he wanted to impress. It was times like this he missed the Gerald Duchane who was heartbroken and withdrawn.

Minutes later, after Duchane had found a mirror and adjusted his shirt properly, a mid-forties woman waltzed in with too much makeup and a sloppily seductive smile. Darr almost wondered if Duchane had found her on some online prostitution site, the way she was dressed. And he decided that must be the answer as soon as the pair started groping each other.

Casting a glare to the floor at his feet, Darr grumbled, "I hate you." He turned and muted his hearing as much as he dared, realizing they weren't taking their affair upstairs just yet.

Fucking hell.

****

"So he's checking on your dad, huh?" Letty summarized later that night, after Ainsley and Britt's cousin had departed. The trio sat on the limited living area furniture, Letty and Izzy on the futon and Britt curled up in the comfy-looking armchair. Guest of honor got first pick of seating, after all.

"Yeah," Izzy said with a nod. She tucked her legs beneath her butt and added lightly, "Or it's Darr's present to Britt."

"Ha ha," Britt returned with a roll of her eyes. "Seriously, Izzy, if you need to go, I'd totally understand."

Izzy shook her head with an easy smile. "No, I'm not worried. Darr's good at what he does." And that was absolutely true. She doubted she'd even seen the extent of his strength. All she knew for sure was that no one lasted long against him.

"Is that a well-rounded truism?" Letty asked suggestively, eyebrows wiggling. "Exactly *how* good is he?"

Britt's eyes went wide. "Izzy, have you slept with him? You have, I'm sure. My God, Izzy!" But her tone wasn't entirely accusatory.

Izzy felt her face redden. "Girls! No!" *Unfortunately.* "No, we haven't slept together. Not ever. Not even a kiss." If she kept going she was sure the disappointment and frustration of that reality would be blatantly apparent.

"Seriously?" Letty asked. "How have you kept that up? I want to jump him after five minutes. Demon or not, that body is—"

"I get it!" Izzy said quickly, holding her hand up to cut off Letty's words. She paused, then, and looked between her friends. She was alone—truly alone—for the first time in a *long* time. It wouldn't last, but … why not take the opportunity? "Honestly," she began on a sigh, "it's not that I haven't wanted to."

Both Letty's and Britt's expressions became curious and they leaned forward. "Go on," Letty urged.

Fighting her embarrassment, Izzy embraced her brief freedom. "There's not much to 'go on' about," she admitted. "And that's the problem. I think I've been hot for him since high school, but of course I couldn't do anything about it." She took a breath and slumped into the back of the futon. "He'll never touch me like that, though."

"You definitely wanted him in high school," Britt offered with a knowing grin.

"How could she not? All those hormones and his sexy body constantly around?" Letty snickered briefly before turning her gaze back to Izzy. "But what's the hold up now? You're an adult, he's still smokin'. I don't see the problem."

Izzy frowned, tears stinging her eyes for the second time that night. The real reason was also the reason she never made a move herself. "It wouldn't be right of me. With the Life Bond, he *has* to stay close and protect me. If he doesn't want me like that, he'd probably fake it just to make life easier for a while." She returned her gaze to her friends and quietly added, "I can't force him into my bed like that." It'd be wrong on every level.

Both women frowned.

"But how do you know he isn't interested?" Letty pushed.

"Couldn't your father release him from the bond?" Britt asked.

Izzy smiled a bit and shook her head. "Why would he be? I'm the face of his servitude, essentially. I'm amazed he doesn't hate me—or he hides it insanely well. And no, a Life Bond is a permanent thing. Breakable only by someone's death."

"Like yours?"

All three jumped at the unfamiliar male voice coming from the back of the cabin. A male figure stepped into the yellow globe light, the sneer on his lips assuring Izzy he wasn't there to make friends.

"How did you get in here?" Britt demanded, pushing to her feet.

"Britt," Izzy called as she and Letty stood as well. Clearly Britt wasn't attuned to identifying demons like Izzy was.

"The usual way," the demon returned. He switched his sneering gaze to Izzy and added, "I don't suppose you're interested in releasing Darr from the ties that bind?"

Izzy swallowed. "If you kill me he'll die, too."

"Supposedly." The demon rushed her without warning, knocking her off her feet and sending her friends diving out of the way.

Izzy crashed over the futon and into a wall, her body aching from the impact. And he'd only hit her with his *hand*. If he summoned a dark energy wave for her she'd be a goner.

"Darr."

Sometime in the first couple of years, Darr had taught her a short, wordless spell she could use to call for him when he wasn't already beside her. He said it sent a jolt through him, alerting his senses to her situation and pulling him to her practically without his consent. She hated using it, but she couldn't let this demon kill her. And he'd surely go for her friends next if he succeeded in killing her. She couldn't let that happen, either.

"Get up," the demon commanded. An invisible hand wrapped around her throat and hauled her mercilessly off the floor. She could barely dig her bare toes into the wood floor. The demon smirked and cocked his head. "Little Izzy Duchane," he taunted, rolling his extended wrist slightly. The force holding her throat rolled to match, straining the side of her neck. "Goodby—"

A strong arm locked around the demon's own throat and threw him bodily backward. The demon rolled several times before his spine met with a wrought iron bedpost.

Darr stalked up to him, his shoulders visibly tight beneath his shirt, fists clenched at his sides. "You *dare*," he growled, his deep voice full of venom and promises of pain.

"W-wait!" the demon begged, pushing to his knees and struggling to stand.

Darr yanked him to his feet and locked a hand around his neck. Izzy couldn't hear what he said next, but she didn't need to. A cold chill swept through the room, the overhead lights flickered, and the demon let out a gurgled scream Izzy could barely hear. Darr released the corpse a moment before it was consumed in black hellfire.

The chill faded. The lighting stabilized.

Izzy pushed herself to her knees, realizing her ankle had twisted when her attacker's concentration had snapped and she'd fallen. But that was the least of her pains. She'd crashed into a metal bar and tumbled into a solid wooden wall, cracking her head and at least one of her shoulders. *He made it...*

"Izzy," Darr called gently, dropping to a knee in front of her as his hands landed on her shoulders. His touch was feather light as he discerned her injuries. "I'm sorry."

The guilt that choked his voice squeezed her heart.

"I'm okay," she insisted. "Just some new bruises. No bikini for me tomorrow."

Darr frowned deeply. He clearly wasn't appreciative of her attempted humor. "I'm going to pick you up," he warned. A heartbeat after she nodded her understanding, he'd swept her into his arms. The movement sent some new jolts of pain through her, but being settled and cradled against his strong, broad chest countered that pain with encompassing warmth.

Izzy groaned faintly and let her head land on his shoulder as he stood.

"Is she okay?" Britt asked quietly from somewhere behind Darr.

"She will be."

"What about ... other demons?" Letty asked hesitantly. "Will there be more?"

"Unlikely," Darr replied as he moved toward Izzy's claimed bed. He stepped right over the new scorch mark on the floor where the other demon had died. He laid her down carefully before lifting his gaze to the two watching women. "Could you give us privacy?" He worded it like a request, but Izzy knew better. The last time she'd been injured—again in his brief absence, no less—he'd nearly blown a hole in her roof. And her then-boyfriend had wasted no time ending things, although she'd been kind of relieved about that part.

"Of course," Britt said, catching Letty's elbow. "Come on, we'll crash with Ainsley tonight."

Letty nodded and after grabbing a change of clothes added, "Take care of her."

As if that needed to be said. If there was one thing Izzy had learned over the years, it was that Darr would always be there for her.

After the door closed behind her friends Darr moved and sat on the edge of the mattress at her side. He brushed some straggling orange-red wisps from her face and said, "Your shoulder is dislocated. I can pop it back into place, but it'll hurt."

Izzy cringed and her head rallied against her for it. Releasing a heavy breath, she said, "Okay, let's get it over with. Then can you get the Aleve from my bag? I hit my head, too."

Darr ran his hand over her head with a frown. Silence ticked between them until he finally said, "Your head should be fine, it's just sore."

He helped Izzy to a sitting position, hovered his hands over her shoulder, and told her to be sure not to bite her tongue. She locked her jaw shut, closed her eyes, and did her best not to scream as searing pain shot through her from her shoulder. It tore at her, lighting her senses on fire for a minute before fading rapidly. "Ah." She gasped when she was sure she wouldn't scream. "Wow, that hurt."

"Does it feel better?" Darr asked, already kneeling before her travel bag.

Izzy hesitated and cautiously rolled her shoulder. It was sore, but it responded immediately, and it didn't hurt nearly as bad. "Yes, thank you," she assured him.

Darr handed her the pills she'd requested and quickly fetched her some water to take them with before sitting again beside her on the bed. "I'm sorry, Izzy. I should have been here."

She opened her mouth to tell him to shove the guilt somewhere he'd never find it again when her brain re-engaged. "My dad! Is he all right?"

It was hard to miss Darr's shudder of horror. And it took a *lot* for her beloved macho demon to shudder for any reason. "That depends. He may be working toward a heart attack, but I refuse to intervene in that."

Izzy knitted her brows. "What?"

Darr shook his head and reached out, resting his hand gingerly over the sore on head. "It's nothing. Nothing suspicious was happening, unless you count his latest companion's attraction to him. You should lie back down."

Izzy did her best not to swoon at the touch and knew he was right. She usually had better control than that. "Ew. Yeah, never mind."

His lips twitched and hers did the same. She let him help her ease down to the pillow and did her best to help him unfold the covers for her. But as he pulled them over her, something stumbled in her chest. She caught his wrist when it was near enough and he stilled immediately.

"Darr," she whispered, locking her gaze with his. "Please stay with me tonight."

He shifted her hold on him until he had cupped her hand between his. "I'll be right beside you."

Izzy smiled and scooted as best she could to one side. "Then get comfy." *Oh yeah, your head's not that bad, dummy. He'll see right through this.* But that didn't necessarily mean he'd decline.

Darr's eyes flicked to the spot she'd made before returning to hers. He said nothing for a long second, his expression unreadable. Then, finally, he replied, "If that's what you want." Izzy watched as he toed off his boots and pulled back the comforter again in order to slide beneath. And she had the silliest realization that his feet probably hung off the bed with how tall he was.

He slipped his arm beneath her neck and gently assured her it was okay to roll into him, which she wasted no time in doing. With her head tucked beneath his jaw and her ear over his heart, Izzy sighed. His scent invaded her nostrils and his steady heartbeat soothed her rattled nerves. Maybe he'd never love her, or even want her, but at least he was good to her. At least she had a few scattered moments like this she could treasure.

"'Night, Darr," she murmured as her consciousness drifted.

He gave her injured shoulder a gentle squeeze and his voice trailed right down her spine, warming her in ways she'd never admit to. "Goodnight, Izzy."
****

Morning had broken, sunlight once again chasing the darkness away, reminiscent of a larger conflict Darr was glad to stay out of. He was sure it was still cold outside, given their elevation, but he couldn't actually feel the chill. His entire body was burning thanks to the sleeping woman in his arms. What the hell had he been thinking, staying in bed with her all night?

He'd been thinking he'd nearly failed her, that's what.

He'd been halfway around the country, practically watching Gerald Duchane getting more action than he himself had had in decades. It was horrifying and humiliating all at the same time. And then Izzy's voice had exploded in his head, the summoning trick he'd taught her so long ago coming into play. He hadn't wasted an extra moment to double-check Gerald's safety before transporting himself to her, and in those precious moments she'd been injured.

If he could kill himself without leaving her unprotected, he'd be sorely tempted to do it.

But his angry thoughts vanished when Izzy's leg slid between his, her thigh and stomach cradling his erection. *Shit.* And she was waking up, too.

Izzy moaned, the sound full of sleep and far too sexy for his own good. A moment later she'd rolled properly into his chest and was blinking her beautiful brown eyes up at him drowsily. It was only then that Darr realized he'd wound both of his arms around her at some point in the night. Dammit.

"Morning," Izzy said with a small, tempting smile. "Thank you … for staying with me."

"You don't need to thank me," he said, hoping she was too asleep to notice the difference in his voice. Damn did he want her. Having her voluptuous body pressed against him was delicious torture.

Izzy frowned and adjusted her arms until she could frame his face in her palms. "I do," she insisted.

Darr pulled in a breath and did his best to will her to back off. But his heart wasn't in it this morning and when her fingers stretched to touch his hair, he snapped. His arms tightened around her and he crushed his lips to hers hungrily.

Izzy moaned against his lips and buried her hands in his hair as she gave into his kiss, even opening her lips for him before he could demand entrance. He took full advantage of the offering and swept his tongue inside, finding she tasted every bit as sweet and enticing as he'd imagined. He tangled one hand in her hair as the other slid down to cup her ass. With one little tug she was rocking against him and sliding her tongue along his simultaneously. The reciprocated desire in her kiss surprised him and made it impossible to pull away.

Darr growled into her kiss, grabbing her top thigh and pulling it over his hip as he rolled her beneath him.

Izzy gasped when he released her lips in order to dip his head and trail kisses down her throat. She responded by curling her arms around his back, holding on and continuing to arch her hips into his rhythmically. Damned woman was going to have him coming in his pants if she kept that up.

Fortunately—or *un*fortunately, whichever the case was—that was when his sensitive ears picked up the sound of Izzy's temporary roommates approaching the cabin.

With a growl of frustration Darr tore his lips from Izzy's neck and rolled off her, leaving his body instantly cold and his dick aching.

Still catching her breath, Izzy rolled onto her side to look at him. "Darr?"

He looked away and sat up, swinging his feet to the floor. "Your friends are coming."

"Oh." Izzy flopped onto her back and from the corner of his eye he saw her chest rise and fall in a long, deep breath. "Damn."

His lips twitched with the urge to grin at their shared sentiments, but instead he turned an arched brow in her direction. She immediately flushed and he had to dig his stubs of nails into his palms to keep from falling on her. Instead he asked, "How's your head?"

Izzy blinked at him for a moment before propping herself up on her elbows and gently prodding around on her head. "Better," she finally said at about the time the key hit the door.

Darr nodded briefly and stood. "I'll be outside if you need me." He grabbed his shoes, doing his best to pretend he didn't see her pout, and vanished as the door swung open.

****

The remnants of a headache and soreness in her shoulder that Izzy had to deal with for most of the rest of the day were nothing compared to the tingling in her lips or the ache between her legs. And she wanted to confide in her two best friends, she really did, but she couldn't. Not on this. Human-demon relationships were generally frowned upon in society and Britt already disliked him as it was. Besides, Izzy was pretty sure Darr wouldn't want it gossiped about. The problem was that on her own Izzy didn't know how to interpret that kiss.

Does it even qualify as a 'kiss'?

It had been so sensually intense, and escalated so quickly, that Izzy felt like they'd practically started at third base. The very memory of his tongue sliding around her mouth, combined with the grinding surge of his hips over hers, or his hand on her butt was enough to send heat pooling low in her belly again. If he popped up in front of her and pinned her to the tree she was leaning against, or the grass she was sitting on, and tried to take her right there in view of everyone at the resort, she wouldn't stop him. Hell, the idea was kind of exciting.

Get a grip, girl. Really, whatever had possessed Darr to react to her like that, she knew in her gut it was a fluke. Maybe it was just a man's 'morning hormones' combined with a terribly long dry spell. She often wondered—or worried, rather—that he spent many of the nights away with another woman while she slept, but the few times she'd prodded for information about what he did in reality hadn't left her with any solid conclusions. To hear him tell it he stayed and simply stood guard in the house all night long. Every single night. All by himself.

"Why aren't you at the beach?"

Izzy jumped a bit, realizing she'd been so lost in thought she hadn't sensed his approach. *How embarrassing.* "Didn't feel like it," she replied on a sigh. Which was about as honest as she could be. She didn't want to say she couldn't stop thinking about their morning, let alone convince her body to get past it.

"Are you feeling all right?" Darr knelt down at her side, the concern in his voice breaking her resolve and pulling her gaze to his.

She could spend all day drowning in those ashen eyes.

Swallowing heavily, Izzy nodded. "I am." She fell silent and the moment became awkward. What should she say? Was he still thinking about their kiss? Did it even mean anything to him?

The brush of his touch startled her back into the moment and she found he was sliding her sleeve back, apparently in order to study her shoulder. Still, the tips of his fingers grazed her bare skin and she fought not to let the shiver show.

"Your shoulder looks good," he said. His gaze lifted back to hers but his hand didn't move. "So what's on your mind?"

Damn him for knowing her so well.

Forcing a semi-smile, Izzy caught his wrist and brought his hand up to cup her cheek. He offered no resistance. "I was … thinking about this morning." Not what she'd meant to say, but she'd always found it so hard to lie to him. And, really, how bad could acknowledging something that had happened be?

Chapter Four

"Why would you do that?"

Izzy didn't really know how to take that question. Was that better or worse than some expression of regret? "Why *wouldn't* I?"

Darr pulled his hand away and rested his knuckles on the grass. "You know why."

Was he serious? Izzy choked on a confused laugh and sat up properly. "No, actually. I really don't."

This time he frowned as if he thought she was being deliberately oblivious. "Izzy, look at the facts. I'm a demon. I'm sworn to protect you from any and all harm, but otherwise we're incompatible."

Her heart lodged in her throat, Izzy swallowed and shoved to her feet. "I refuse to accept that." She spun on her heel, not wanting to see the frustration her response would surely generate. Not wanting him to see the tears she was fighting back. Now she wished she had gone down to the lakeshore with her friends. Playing in the sun and the cool water despite her once-raging headache would surely have been better than this.

A strong hand latched onto her wrist as she started up the wooden steps to the cabin. "Izzy."

Closing her eyes and releasing a breath, Izzy forced herself to turn to face him. She owed it to him—and probably herself—to hear him out. Only he wasn't interested in talking, apparently.

Darr closed the distance between them with one large step, releasing her wrist in favor of sliding one hand behind her head and anchoring the other on her butt in order to lift her to his lips. Like earlier, his kiss was demanding. He took full possession of her mouth, sweeping his tongue inside and stroking hers in a rhythm that had her aching all over again.

Izzy moaned and gave in to the kiss, shoving her confusion aside. This was what she wanted. His taste, his touch, his passion, she wanted all of it. So she looped her arms around his neck and locked her legs around his waist. Through the denim of her cutoffs and the denim of his black jeans she could feel his arousal. He was just as hard as he'd been that morning and that knowledge only made her want him more.

Darr groaned and moved forward, and the next thing Izzy knew, they were toppling onto her bed. He rolled until she landed over his chest, a hand on her thigh keeping her legs around him. He released her butt and trailed that hand up her spine, sending delicious shivers through her body even as his hips bucked in time to another stroke of his masterful tongue. She rocked her own hips forward encouragingly, trying to catch his tongue with hers.

She broke the kiss when his tongue slipped free of hers again, and she opted to trail her tongue along his jaw, enjoying the poorly-stifled moan that rose up in his chest. Licking and nipping until she reached his ear, Izzy whispered, "How about I show you how compatible we are?"

His hips bucked a little harder in response and she took that as a good sign. With a teasing nip on his earlobe, Izzy sat up, still straddling him, and sought out his gaze. As soon as she found it, she lifted her shirt over her head, revealing the emerald bikini top she'd worn the day before.

Darr growled almost possessively and his hands burned invisible trails up her sides until he'd found the tie to her top. One sharp tug released it and he tossed it away with one hand while capturing a breast in his other.

Izzy moaned low and rocked into his touch, throwing her head back as he palmed her breast. He caught the other breast and synchronized his touch, squeezing and molding all while his hips continued to buck up beneath her. And God how she wished they could just unzip their respective jeans and take that final step, but her swimsuit bottoms would still be in the way. Not to mention whatever he might wear beneath his own pants. But his touch on her chest had set her aflame and she couldn't be denied.

Her hands dragged down his chest, earning low growls and groans, before landing on his belt buckle and quickly releasing it. When she tugged his zipper free, his hands receded and she had just enough time to wonder if he was chickening out before he flipped her over, coming to kneel behind her and hooking his fingers into her shorts.

Izzy's cheeks flushed as she realized what position he intended to take her in, but she couldn't deny the thrill of it. She'd never made love in this position and it seemed appropriate that he'd be the one to change that.

Darr let the denim scrape her skin as he dragged it down—along with the bikini bottoms—until it was gone, tossed aside somewhere. The bed dipped when he returned and he guided her hips up with one hand. Another hand slipped between her thighs and urged them apart. When he was satisfied, he leaned over her, the hand on her hips sliding up to catch one of her breasts again and tug at her nipple.

"There's no going back from this, Izzy," he warned, his delicious voice thick with need. Just the sound of it made her core pulse demandingly.

"Take a deep breath, Darr," she whispered, arcing her butt into him for emphasis. "I want this. I'm ready."

She gasped at the pinch on her nipple and nearly missed the mouth that latched onto her shoulder.

He trailed wet, hungry kisses down her spine, his hands following at her sides until one of them dipped again between her thighs. And this time he went for gold, one finger slipping inside her as his thumb pressed on her nub. Izzy gasped loudly and rocked her hips, her body begging him to do that again. He inserted a second finger, plunging them deeper and adjusting the pressure on her nub. He flicked, repeated his previous motion, and Izzy cried out as pleasure erupted inside her.

But Darr didn't give her any time to recover, removing his hand and grabbing hold of her hips before surging into her center mid-climax.

Izzy screamed as ecstasy erupted inside her, blurring her vision and making her weak for a long moment. She was aware of Darr moving, rocking, and shallowly thrusting behind her. Working her body back up to a state of desperation in record time.

"Oh," she moaned as he sank deeper again. Her hips reflexively rolled backward, into him, as her senses came back to her. "Mmm," she hummed, her hands digging into the sheets beneath her.

Darr leaned over her again, releasing one hip in order to balance his weight while he continued pumping into her. "Let me hear you," he rumbled, his lips somewhere over her spine near the nape of her neck. He emphasized his command by driving in deeper.

Izzy made another sound somewhere between gasp and moan and ground her butt into his pelvis, her body desperate to take him deeper. "Harder," she begged breathlessly. "Please."

He trailed his tongue down her spine until he was sitting up behind her again, reclaimed her hips, and surged home with more force than ever before. And when Izzy cried out in pleasure, he did it again.

She could feel her second orgasm coming and her breathing doubled. "Darr!"

He growled, reached around her, and did something indecipherable to her clit at the same time as he thrust into her. White light exploded behind her eyes and Izzy distantly heard her own voice crying out as her body rocked with the force of her orgasm.

****

Darr held Izzy close as she slept, her body needing to restore its energy after three explosive orgasms in a row. His own demonic heart was still beating wildly in his chest. He hadn't anticipated his own reaction, let alone hers. One minute he'd been concerned that her injuries were causing her pain and the next minute he was kissing her again. He barely even remembered what they'd said to each other in between. But he did remember that her obvious distractedness had been because of him and the morning they'd shared.

A morning that didn't come close to comparing to their afternoon. It was like something had snapped inside him, and when she'd wrapped her legs around his hips, their fate was sealed. He needed to have her, naked and writhing beneath him, and nothing was going to stop him. The only problem was, now that he had a taste of her he doubted he'd be able to contain himself in the future. He'd be aching for her again in an hour he was sure.

He was so distracted he nearly missed the sounds of Britt and the others approaching the cabin. *Shit.*

Carefully easing out of Izzy's arms, Darr melded with the shadows around him to quickly pull his clothes on. He'd just finished adjusting the comforter around her shoulders—her clothes conveniently hidden by the comforter as well—when the cabin door swung open.

"Feeling better…" Britt said as she led the way inside.

Britt and Letty stopped just inside the cabin, the other two opting to wait out on the porch.

Darr held a finger to his lips and gestured toward the door. They took his lead, stepped out, and he stopped in the doorway.

"Is she okay?" Letty asked quietly.

Darr nodded. "She's just tired. She didn't sleep well last night."

"We're going to grab dinner," Britt said. "Won't she want to eat?"

Probably. Swallowing his sigh, Darr said, "I'll wake her. She'll be out in a couple of minutes if she's up for it." Which he was sure she would be, but he chose to embrace his reputation of being overprotective in order to further his little lie. Because the last rumor he wanted to spread about the woman he protected was that she was also sleeping with a demon. *As if she doesn't have a big enough target on her back.*

Closing the cabin door, Darr turned and made his way back to the bed. He could sense Izzy was already stirring.

He knelt by the bed and brushed some red wisps from her face, whispering, "Time to get up."

Izzy groaned and stretched, flopping onto her back and arching in the process. The comforter barley covered her rosy nipples and his dick throbbed. But this time he fought the urge and instead held his position, waiting for her to wake up fully.

"Darr? What is it?" Her voice was sleepy, but he could tell her memory was functioning by the adorable pink flush on her cheeks. She rolled back onto her side, facing him, and tugged the comforter up just a bit.

"Your friends wanted to know if you were planning on joining them for dinner," he replied. Jerking a thumb to the door, he added, "They're outside."

Her eyes went wide and her head snapped toward the lone digital clock beside Letty's bed. "Oh my God!" She scrambled up, not pausing until she noticed her clothes beside her. Looking back to him, she asked, "What're these doing here?"

He couldn't stop the grin. "I didn't think you wanted your friends to know what we did this afternoon. If I was wrong, I'm happy to correct that." There were all sorts of fun ways he could make her friends squirm, really. Not that he disliked them, he just didn't feel like sharing Izzy's company at the moment. Not now that he'd gotten such a good taste of her.

Lifting the top to her swimsuit, Izzy chucked it at his head. "You will do no such thing!" She scrambled from the bed, shirt and shorts in one hand, and moved toward her borrowed dresser.

Darr lifted the swim top and grinned. "Thanks for the memento."

Izzy paused, fresh pair of panties in hand, and looked back at him. And then she groaned. "Wow, I never pegged you for being such a *guy*."

As she rushed through dressing for a public appearance Darr stood. "You thought I was what, then? A robot?"

"No, of course not," Izzy replied as she zipped up her shorts. "I just ... I don't know, I didn't figure you were the trophy type."

Darr stepped into her space and spun her around before she could tug her shirt over her head. With a hand at the small of her back and another tangled in her hair he pulled her close and, their noses touching, he said, "In case you've forgotten, Izzy, I *am* a demon. I may know how to play civilized, but I'm a violent ass at heart."

The smile she offered him destroyed his argument easier than a sword might destroy wet paper. "Sure you are, Mr. Bad-Ass." She pressed her lips to his and slipped from his grip. "But you're lying to one of us I'm afraid."

He snorted and tossed her swimsuit top to the bed. "Sure I am. You know I'll be trailing you tonight."

"You trail me every night," Izzy returned, tearing a quick brush through her hair. It made the usual god-awful ripping sound and he cringed as she winced.

"Slower," he instructed on reflex, moving up behind her.

"Kinda in a hurry," Izzy returned. One more horrid rip later she set the brush back down and grinned up at him. "Besides, I'm done. Now remember, Britt wants you out of her line of sight."

With an incline of his head, Darr replied, "I remember." He pressed a kiss to the top of her head and stepped into a late-afternoon shadow obligingly.
****

Izzy tossed the blankets aside as she startled awake sometime that night. Her heart was still racing wildly in her chest and she rested a hand over it as if the motion would settle her pulse. Or her breathing.

Darr…

He was often the focus of her dreams, it was true, but this one had been different. In this one she'd been blatantly manipulating his tie to her to keep him in her bed. And it wasn't until they'd gotten in a nasty fight and he'd declared that he wished she would just kill herself then, that Izzy had finally been jarred awake. *What does that mean?*

Earlier that very day, after years of silently yearning for him, they'd finally been intimate. And the reality of his prowess in the bedroom obliterated all her favorite fantasies. She wanted to be on cloud nine—proverbially, of course—but her heart hesitated. What if her dream was telling her something? What if her dream was trying to tell her that Darr was—or would come to be—seeing their affair as her abuse of their bond?

What if she got so desperate someday that she really *did* threaten to kill herself to keep him with her?

No. She couldn't imagine herself doing that, let alone doing that to him. She'd have released him from their bond years ago if it was within her power. But maybe he didn't really know that. *Should I tell him my feelings?* Or would her saying that come off as manipulation somehow?

Or, worse … what if Darr was the one manipulating her?

Her throat constricted at the thought and she struggled to take a deep breath. No, surely that wasn't it. That seemed as inconceivable as her deliberate manipulation of him. But still … the very fact that these thoughts existed in her mind somewhere had to be a sign of something. Perhaps she'd been right before about resisting a relationship with him. Or perhaps it just needed to be talked about.

Glancing at the digital display beside Letty's bed which read two-thirty-three, Izzy sighed and swung her feet around. She clearly wasn't going back to sleep just yet, so it was time to find her demon.

But as soon as her feet hit the floor something cold and slimy wrapped around her ankles and tugged sharply.

Izzy cried out in shock and instinctive terror, flying forward and slamming hard onto the old floor. The demon under her bed continued to tug, dragging her into the darkness—and to who knew where after that.

"Darr!"

Chapter Five

Darr watched the stars twinkle overhead almost mockingly. Tiny, little pinpricks of bright, clean light obscuring the surrounding darkness. At least the moon was only a sliver of itself tonight.

The resort was quiet, as was befitting of the hour. Even the waves of the lake were minimal, contributing to the deafening silence around him. Barely any creatures dared rustle about in his vicinity. Animals—even insects—were instinctively attuned to beings of darkness. Maybe the silence was why he disliked being outside at night. Or maybe it was just worse tonight because of the passion he and Izzy had shared earlier that day.

Just the memory of their afternoon was enough to get him hard again. And now that he had a taste of her on his tongue, he had a serious problem. Demons were naturally inclined toward vices of all variety and, in Darr's case, he had recently deduced his was addiction. A very specific addiction, too. Now, leaning against the tree nearest Izzy's window, Darr could barely drag his thoughts from her. He didn't want to be stuck outside, he wanted to be stretched out next to her in that small bed. Or preferably on top of her, working out every kind of moan she could possibly make.

Shit.

They had one more night at this accursed resort. One more night where she'd be sharing her living—and sleeping—space with others. One more night he'd be relegated to the outside just to be within screaming distance of her. She'd offered to reserve him a cabin of his own, of course, but he'd declined. It wasn't like he needed a cabin of his own when he didn't actually sleep.

Hell, he didn't need a cabin or a bed at all. He just wanted to be in there with her.

"*Darr!*"

The scream was muffled, half reaching his ears and half firing the burning alarm in his head that triggered when she summoned him. But she'd never summoned him in quite such a terrified way and he was instantly furious.

How dare some scum scare her like that.

The shadows parted as he appeared in the cabin, barely sparing a glance at Izzy's startled friends. His stomach hit the floor when he saw Izzy's hands slip beneath the bed. His mind roared and with barely a flick of his wrist, the entire bed, from frame to top sheet, when flying. But Izzy was gone. Sucked into the shadows in a way only another demon could manage.

He tried reopening the same passageway, but in the middle of the night such a feat was nearly impossible. The more prevalent the shadows, the harder it was to follow one.

His fist hit the floor, shattering the fake wood laminate. He bit back the shout of fury that clawed at his chest. He could feel his power building, fueled by his rage and the unfamiliar twinge of fear. *Fear.* Something he hadn't felt now in over two decades, also—if indirectly—thanks to Izzy.

"Ohmygod," Britt breathed behind him. "She's … she's gone…"

The woman's words settled like concrete in his gut.

Izzy was gone. In the hands of a demon he hadn't even glimpsed. And he was no tracker. His power was muscle, not something that required more finesse like tracking. But he *had* to find her. Had to find her before the demon did whatever it had planned. And for that he was going to need help.

****

Izzy emptied her stomach the moment she finally landed on solid ground.

She'd never been in that other dimension for so long. Whenever Darr transported her through the shadows it was always fast, most of the time it was instantaneous. But this … this had felt like hours. Even now, with her dinner and late-night snack on the ground, her stomach heaved dangerously. Her head still swimming, Izzy did her best to look around, but the space she was kneeling in was so dark she could barely discern the walls around her.

"You must be sweet little Isolde Duchane," an unfamiliar male voice declared. His voice echoed in the darkness around her, seeming to come from everywhere at once. She didn't imagine even the most stubbornly naïve person would have mistaken that voice for anything other than that of a demon. A dangerous, dangerous demon.

Glaring straight ahead, Izzy snapped, "You mean you kidnapped me without even knowing who I am?" Seriously?

"Of course not," the voice assured her. He was behind her now.

Izzy shoved to her feet and spun, but even her long hair didn't seem to hit anything. Her reaction only served to throw the world out of orbit again.

"I ordered another to grab you," he continued. Behind her again.

This time Izzy held still despite the chill that raked her spine. She could've sworn she felt his breath that time. "What do you want with me?" *Is this about Dad?* Had whoever might have been going after him noticed Darr there last night? Or was this about the other thing, the demon who'd attacked her?

The demon in the room with her made a thoughtful sound, his hum sounding from her left this time. She reflexively turned her glare that way but, naturally, his voice came from the opposite direction when he finally responded. "You are my pawn. My ticket, even. You, little Isolde, are bait."

"Bait?" That was the most ludicrous thing in the world. She wasn't close enough to her father for that to be an obvious tactic—though she supposed she shouldn't rule it out, either. He *was* the reason she'd needed a demon bodyguard after all. *Or…?* Or was this about Darr?

"You look like you're starting to catch on."

Narrowing her eyes and slowly turning her head wide, Izzy said, "And I bet you have a stupid arrogant smirk on your face right now. So what? What the hell do you mean I'm 'bait'?"

"How rude of me." There was a pause and he whispered his next words directly into her face, yet she never saw a thing.

It was terrifying.

"I am Creed. And I've come for what's mine."

****

"Well this is unusual," Zahk stated as he stepped into the room. His dark gaze swept over the mess briefly, lingered on the two pajama-clad women gathered on the farthest bed, and landed on Darr. "What's with the summoning?"

Darr released a breath, wondering for the umpteenth time in the past ten minutes if this was really a good idea. But he had no other choice. Nothing he'd tried had worked. "I need your help."

Zahk arched a brow in silent curiosity.

With more effort than he imagined he was able to muster, Darr admitted, "Izzy's been … taken. I can't find where."

"Ouch." Zahk pulled his hands from his pockets and his gaze flicked to the scorch mark from the first demon's attack. "Who'd you kill?"

"Another attacker. Last night." And Darr very much doubted the coincidence of that. Someone was after Izzy and sending lesser demons to do the dirty work. Which meant whoever it was had at least marginal respect for his strength.

"Two?" Zahk questioned, turning his attention back to Darr.

"Can you help? You're the only one I trust." There was no sense in not laying all his cards on the table. Zahk would understand. Even if that was only really because he was under the impression Darr's physical life was on the line.

Zahk pursed his lips and looked to where Izzy's bed was supposed to be. "I'll do what I can," he said. He moved and knelt at the edge of the dust that hadn't been swept out from under the bed. "Nasty," he muttered as he slowly waved a stretched-out palm over the space.

Darr watched from where he stood, aware that what Zahk was doing required concentration. He didn't know if Zahk was actually skilled in tracking, but he had to try. He hadn't been lying about Zahk being the only one he could call on. Letty, however, didn't seem to recognize the need for stillness. She removed herself from Britt's side and stepped up to Darr's as quietly as she was able—which wasn't much, between the squeaky floors and a human's naturally heavier footfalls.

"Can he find her?" she whispered, concern in her voice. It was probably in her scent, too, if Darr bothered to look.

"Quiet." He didn't know if Zahk could find her. Nor did he feel like voicing that doubt.

"Well," Zahk said with a heavy breath as he sat back on his haunches. "I can sense the demon's residual energy, but not much else. He went deep."

Darr opened his mouth to ask for more, but Britt's shrill exclamation cut him off.

"Deep? You mean she's in *Hell*?" The idea clearly terrified her. As well it should have, since a human couldn't survive in Hell.

"No," Zahk said with a shake of his head. He stood. "I think Darr would've been able to sense if this was a portal to Hell. She's on Earth. She just spent a while in limbo first."

"Limbo?" Letty asked.

"Our word for the dimension we travel through," Darr offered shortly. "Between the shadows."

"I don't understand," Britt said, sounding strained. Darr didn't bother to look at her. "You can tell where she *was*, but not where she *is*?"

"We're all connected to limbo," Zahk explained. "Where she went when it opened on the other end, though, that's anyone's guess."

Dammit. Darr's fists clenched tight at his sides. "Do you know any trackers?"

"None you'd trust."

Touché. And that was a fucking problem. "What about ones *you* trust?" He was going to have to make an exception somewhere.

Zahk's eyes widened for a beat and he whistled. "You're really still insisting Old Duchane managed to bind you, huh?"

Darr snapped a glare at his supposed friend. "This really isn't the time for that. Or do you want me dead?"

"Hey, easy," Zahk said, holding his hands up in a surrendering gesture. "I didn't mean it that way. I can make a couple calls, see if anyone good's available. It'll just take a minute or three."

"You have one."

Another brow arched, Zahk asked, "And then what?"

Not having a real answer, Darr replied, "Then I get desperate." It was the best truth he had.

Zahk scoffed and moved toward the door. "I'll be outside for a moment, then."

But he never made it to the door. All the shadows in the room began to spin and gather over the scorch mark on the floor. Letty darted back to the bed and Britt, both girls whimpering in fear. Zahk turned in place but made no move to step closer. Darr held his ground, hoping against all logic it was Izzy.

****

"You should really keep a closer eye on your toys, Darr," Creed declared coldly as Izzy dry heaved behind him. She officially *hated* the way he—or his invisible companion—teleported.

But at least she'd managed to convince the creep to return her. Or give her a chance at returning.

She suspected Creed thought he was just dangling his bait in front of his prey, but Izzy knew better. Darr would save her.

When she finally managed to lift her swaying gaze to Darr, however, what she saw stalled her heart in her chest. He looked frozen, his ash-gray eyes wider than usual and his whole body uncharacteristically tense. Almost like he was … afraid. But it passed quickly and then his fury was back, raw and rising in his narrowed eyes. In a flash he went from frozen to lunging, a nearly invisible energy coiling around the fist he'd pulled back.

Instinct kicking in, Izzy sprang to her feet and bolted for the girls. It was best to get on the other side of an attack like that. Not until Britt and Letty were reaching for her did she even register Zahk, standing beside the door.

Drywall and wood paneling exploded as Darr's demonic energy blast fired. Dust and smoke filled the space in a loud outburst that had Izzy and her friends clamping hands over their ears and ducking. She'd *never* seen him attack like that.

Creed's echoing laughter seeped through the smoke. "You'll never hit me with an attack so untrained. I'd have thought you knew that by now."

What? She'd guessed Creed and Darr must have had a history, but she was increasingly worried about what that history was. They must have always been enemies. Or perhaps they'd once been friendly and Creed had betrayed Darr… She supposed that could explain it, too. She just hoped she got the chance to ask him about it.

"You made a mistake coming to me," Darr threatened a yard or three ahead.

The smoke began to clear and Izzy strained her eyes to see through it. She was hoping to see Darr, but her eyes landed first on Zahk. He'd stepped forward slightly, as if he wanted a better view. His attention seemed focused on the struggle. *Why isn't he helping?* He was supposed to be Darr's friend. She'd never gotten to know him, but they'd interacted a little now and then. She remembered how happy she'd felt to learn Darr had at least one friend he could keep in touch with from his old life—a life he never talked about.

"Can't you do something?" she called, crawling forward on the bed.

Zahk looked over to her, his expression solemn. "Darr wouldn't want me to."

Whether she liked it or not that was certainly true. It would probably be an insult to his pride, not just as her protector, but as a man. As a demon. She certainly knew that demons had their vanities.

Darr crashed hard onto the splintered floor, skidding back nearly to Zahk's feet, and Creed stepped just inside the hole in the wall.

Izzy's heart leapt to her throat and she reacted on instinct. She vaulted from the bed and landed on her knees beside her lover. "Darr!"

"Stay back!"

"No need," Creed called calmly. "I'm not going to kill either of you just yet. This is your warning. Not only have I found you, Darr, but I am going to kill you slowly. This is just the start." The shadows surrounding him sprang up and seemed to smash him into the ground, leaving a vacant space where he'd stood just moments before.

"What, what in the *hell* happened in here?" The horrified demand came from Ainsley. The fight hadn't exactly been muted.

Izzy turned her attention away then, not caring who responded or what was said. "Darr," she called, more softly. She rested a hand on his shoulder and squeezed. The gesture was as much meant to offer comfort as it was to reassure herself. "Are you hurt?"

Jaw tight, Darr lifted his gaze to her. "I should be asking you that. I'm sorry, Izzy."

Trying to offer him the best smile she could, Izzy replied, "Hey, I've got bones of steel. I'm fine."

Darr grunted something incorrigible and tugged her into his chest, one large hand tangled in her hair. With his lips grazing her ear he said, "I'll never let him lay another finger on you."

Izzy opened her mouth to ask about Creed and the myriad of questions dancing around in her head, but she thought better of it at the last moment. They had an audience. It wasn't the right time. So instead she curled her arms around his neck and held tight, taking deep, stabilizing breaths of his scent. At least he was okay, and she was back in his arms. Everything else could wait its turn.

"My wall! What in the name of heaven happened to my wall?" Izzy didn't recognize the voice and Darr immediately stiffened around her.

"We are *so* sorry," Britt said quickly, moving up near Izzy's side. "We'll repay you for all the—"

"No." The shorter, balding man cut her off with a hard look. A look Izzy had learned was actually a cover for uncomfortable fear. Not that the distinction mattered in this case. "I want you all out immediately. No refunds. I'll need the money for this. But I won't call the police if you don't fight it. I don't care who or what brought the demons, but there are no *demon brawls* here, do you understand?"

Izzy swallowed, guilt flaring bright in her chest. No matter what had happened to her, they were supposed to be there for Britt. And she'd gone and ruined her friend's bachelorette party in a spectacular way.

Taking their silence as agreement, the man continued. "You have an hour. I want you off the property in an hour."

"But…" Britt stuttered, clearly at a loss for words. Understandably so.

"Please," Izzy interrupted, reluctantly pushing to her feet and stepping forward. "This is my fault entirely. I have money, I can pay for everything. And I'll leave. No more demons will come after I'm gone." Maybe she could salvage some tiny fragment of Britt's party.

Meeting her stare angrily, he replied, "Then I'll get your information and come after you for the overages."

Behind her, Darr stood, his body language angry. He didn't generally tolerate people talking to her in what he judged a negative, insulting manner. The property owner's words definitely qualified. But Izzy put a hand on his nearest arm to hold him in place.

"Please," she tried again, softening her stare.

"So help me," he interrupted. "I'm well within my rights if I want to call the police and press charges."

"You would be," yet another new voice, also male and undeniably powerful, declared calmly. A moment later a tall, dark-haired, blue-eyed man with perfectly tanned skin stepped through the hole and walked past the owner. "But such extremities aren't necessary. Go back to bed."

Izzy held her breath as a glaze seemed to overtake the owner's eyes and his shoulders slumped. "You're right. I'm sorry. Have a good night." Without another word of explanation he turned and walked off.

The newcomer strode several feet into the cabin before coming to a stop. He was nearly as tall as Darr, Izzy realized, and she was sure he had remarkable power just as she was sure he was *not* a demon. The sensation was confusing. As was Darr's tensing, let alone when he grabbed her arm and tugged her back. Not behind him, but back, so that he *could* pull her behind him if necessary. She was familiar with the stance and instantly on alert.

Now what?

"Infernal shit," Zahk exclaimed from behind her. Izzy flicked a glance back to him only to find he was already gone. Apparently he hadn't wanted to share air-space with the newcomer.

"Um…?" Letty asked hesitantly.

The stranger turned his piercing gaze toward Britt, Letty, and the other women who'd gathered inside during the exchange with the owner. "Why don't you ladies take shelter in the other cabin?" He phrased it like a suggestion but Izzy realized quickly it wasn't.

"Yeah," Britt said slowly, clearly uncomfortable. "Sure…" She looked over at Izzy hesitantly and Izzy smiled.

"I'll be fine." In truth she had *no* idea what the hell was going on, let alone if she would be okay. Despite her faith in Darr, this new guy oozed so much power she was genuinely frightened. And she didn't want her friends anywhere near that.

No one in the room spoke until the door closed behind Britt and the others moments later. Darr remained stationary, like a rock in front of her. Izzy did her best to keep breathing normally. And then the blown-out hole in the wall became solid again, taking with it the damages to the floor. Even the scorch disappeared.

"What…?" How was that *possible*? Unless… *Oh my God…*

Could this guy be Satan?

Chapter Six

"Who are you?" Izzy demanded before she could clamp her mouth shut. She didn't need to see his face to know Darr did *not* approve. Hell, *she* didn't approve. But it was too late for that.

The man met her gaze easily, his expression entirely unreadable. Or bored. It was impossible to tell. "I am Kai."

"What do you want?" Darr interrupted. This guy—Kai—clearly made him uncomfortable.

Kai's eyes narrowed almost imperceptibly when he switched his attention to Darr. Izzy got the distinct impression Darr's clear dislike of him was mutual. "One of my enemies was here moments ago," Kai replied plainly. "I'd hoped to catch him while he was on Earth, but he sensed me coming. Still, he wanted something from you. I need to know what that is."

Izzy gaped. She could only assume Kai had been referring to Creed—a point in his favor—but she couldn't believe his arrogance.

"It's not that complicated," Darr returned. "He wants me dead."

Kai's gaze returned to Izzy. "And you are the demon's weakness."

Izzy swallowed as Darr stepped more properly in front of her. "She's a victim in this."

"Agreed," Kai said. "Stand down, demon. I've no intention of killing you tonight. You could prove useful, and your loyalty to the human woman is … admirable." He definitely hadn't liked praising Darr, whether because he was a demon or just because he didn't often dole out praise was another question.

"Wait," Izzy interrupted, moving to Darr's other side in an effort to stay in the conversation. She looked between them and settled on Kai. He at least seemed willing to answer questions. "I'm confused. You're not a demon, and you're not … human. So what are you?" 'Human' wasn't what she'd wanted to say, but she was uncomfortable using any reference to Satan out loud. And she didn't want to risk upsetting Kai.

Kai looked back to Darr with a question of his own. "She doesn't know?"

Darr released a breath but didn't otherwise relax. Nor did he take his glare off their guest. "He's an angel."

Izzy stumbled back and Darr's hand shot out to catch her by the elbow. She knew she'd been more than a little disoriented earlier, but apparently it hadn't worn off after all. Because Darr hadn't *really* just said 'angel.' Right? "What?"

"I am an angel," Kai echoed firmly. "A warrior."

Oh man... He'd said it, too. Or she was still hallucinating. "This is crazy," she muttered, stepping up to Darr and twisting her hands in his shirt for support. "I think I'm hallucinating. I think I need to lie down. I swear you said *angel*."

"Trust me," Darr replied, curving his arm around her. "I don't like it, either. But you're not hallucinating."

"But…" But what? What was the right question to ask? The right question to start with? *Was* there a 'right question'?

"We may meet again," Kai declared. "If you wish to stay alive, stay out of my line of fire when that time comes. Creed will return for you and I for him. If you choose to warn him, I'll strike you down on the spot."

And with that he was gone in flash of pure, white light.
****

"Angels are *real*?" Izzy repeated for the hundredth time the next morning. She'd barely touched her breakfast.

After Kai's disappearance, and in light of everything that had happened, Izzy had allowed Darr to talk her into coming home. She'd been so exhausted she was practically asleep on her feet for the short time it took her to pack and apologize to Britt, and she'd been sound asleep by the time he tucked her into her bed. Given what she'd been through—just that he knew of— Darr figured she'd be starving when she woke up, so he'd prepared a good breakfast.

Izzy had had other ideas of what to do with her morning, of course. He wasn't surprised, but he sure as hell wasn't in the mood to be grilled about Creed and angels. Although, honestly, he'd take the angel talk over the Creed talk any day. Fortunately she was more focused on that, too.

"Yes," he repeated. "Eat before the food gets cold."

Dramatically stabbing her fork into her chopped potato bites, Izzy rambled, "Why didn't you tell me earlier? Wouldn't angels and demons be natural enemies, then? So why didn't he attack?" She proceeded to stuff the potatoes into her mouth, muffling whatever might have come next.

Darr sighed and sat back in his chair. "That's a long, complicated story. The simple answers are that I didn't tell you because I try *very* hard to stay out of it. We are natural enemies and I have no real clue why he didn't attack. I can't imagine he's that desperate for bait."

Izzy's hand stilled over her plate and she swallowed heavily. "Actually," she said, voice calmed, "that reminds me. Creed … he was going to hold onto me. He said he wanted to use me as 'bait,' for you." He could hear the question in her words and he struggled to hide the cringe.

It was time, then.

"I'm sorry, Izzy," he started. "Creed and I … we have a long, sordid history of mutual hatred. And I imagine it pissed him off when he lost track of me after your father's summoning."

Izzy frowned. "So you were actively fighting each other?"

Darr shook his head. "Nothing so straightforward." She cocked an orange brow and he added, "He was my master."

Silence stretched between them for a long minute as Izzy released the fork entirely. At length she finally asked, "You mean, like … mentor or something … right?" It was clear in her voice that she was more hoping than asking.

Darr shook his head again. "I was his slave, not his pupil." Creed didn't have pupils or apprentices. Well, unless 'for dinner' came at the end of the thought.

Hands flying over her mouth and eyes immediately watering, Izzy jumped from her spot and rounded the table until she'd properly squirmed her way onto his lap. How the hell she'd managed to do that, he wasn't sure, but having her unexpectedly pressing against him in a tight embrace wasn't something he intended to complain about.

"Oh, Darr," she mumbled into his hair. "I'm so sorry. I had no idea."

"I know," he assured her, wrapping his arms tight around her waist. "And I swear, Izzy, I'll never let him touch you again."

Izzy eased back until she was framing his jaw in her hands. "I know." She leaned forward, then, and pressed her lips tenderly over his. But he wasn't in the mood for tender after the night they'd had.

The moment her lips grazed his, Darr's blood burst into flames and he growled, tugging her impossibly close and angling his head to better devour her mouth. His tongue stroked hers firmly and she moaned, threading her fingers through his hair. He kissed her deeply, fervently, until he'd sucked the oxygen from her lungs.

As he released her from his kiss, he swept an arm out and shoved the plates from the table, letting them crash to the floor in a clattering mess. With his other hand he caught her ass and lifted her to the table top.

Izzy laughed lightly, her breathing unstable, and caught the collar of his shirt in a loose grip as he leaned over her. "You're so cleaning that up," she teased.

"Later," he rumbled, already working on her shorts. In no time he'd tugged them down and off and his cock pulsed with need as she willingly spread her legs for him. Latching his lips to the side of her throat, Darr's hands landed on her hips and slipped beneath the sides of her panties. His thumb dipped between her thighs at the same time as he nipped at her flesh and Izzy moaned low. The sound went straight to his cock.

Finding her already more than a little wet, Darr growled against her skin and jerked his hands apart. The motion, combined with his physical strength, snapped her soft, pink panties with ease.

Izzy shook with laughter and he caught her covered breast in one palm, molding the pliant flesh roughly. He needed a taste of her so badly he was nearly bursting.

His other hands landed on the inside of her thighs, parting them a bit more, and he dropped to his knees. He heard Izzy suck in a sharp breath when she realized his intent and one of his hands dipped beneath the hem of her shirt again. Searching and massaging, earning another delicious moan from her mouth. Then he found his target with his mouth, letting his tongue tease her folds as he lapped at her juices.

One of Izzy's hands immediately tangled in his hair, holding on tight, and her hips rolled a little closer. He took the opportunity to slip his tongue into her wet heat and tried not to growl again at the sounds she made in response. He licked and stroked and nipped as deeply, as hard as he could. As hard as he dared. And when he sensed she was on the edge he plunged two fingers deep into her core while switching his lips to her clit and sucking hard.

Izzy screamed out her orgasm, her body bucking sharply before she collapsed back on the table. Probably thinking he was done.

Instead Darr pushed to his feet, unbuckled and unzipped his pants, and let his hardened dick pop free. With a grunt and a long, leisurely stroke of his hands down her sides, he tugged her hips forward as he thrust into her tight core. She was hot and soaked and so fucking tight he nearly came on the spot. The surprised, ecstasy-laden gasp that tore from her didn't help.

She moaned again, her back arching as she took him in. Her legs lifted and locked around his hips as her hands curled into the table top, seeking purchase. "Darr," she breathed, gasping for breath as he pumped into her relentlessly.

Darr shut out the world around them as he took her, filling her to the limit every time. Her pelvis rocked against his balls and his hands slid up again, seeking his own purchase. He found her breasts and pulled them free of her bra, still under her shirt, in order to play with her nipples.

Izzy moaned her appreciation, bucking harder against him. "Yes!"

He ground his teeth in an effort to control himself at least enough not to actually hurt her and gave her nipples a hard flick. Izzy's nails dug into his forearms and he thrust into her with more strength than he'd meant to.

Another pleasure-filled scream tore from Izzy just moments before his own orgasm slammed into him, ripping a guttural cry of his own from his lungs.

He nearly collapsed to the floor before his senses returned to him, and he gently pulled out of her, her legs falling limply to dangle off the table. He had to brace his weight with both hands just to stay on his feet.

Izzy's voice was breathless when she finally said, "Thank you for breakfast."

****

Izzy would bet money her father had never considered that his little girl would fall in love with a demon. Let alone the very same demon he'd summoned to protect her. And she was *sure* her father would flip a lid if he somehow learned she and her demon had had hot, carnal sex on the dining room table he'd purchased for her a few years back.

The knowledge *almost* tempted her to tell him. Not that she would of course. What girl wanted her father knowing anything about her sex life?

Still, there was one other thought that popped up in her mind while she was toweling off after a late-morning shower. In all the chaos of the night before, Izzy hadn't had an opportunity to talk to Darr about their circumstance. About her feelings. She still wanted to, possibly even more so now, but she was hesitant. There were a hundred ways it could go wrong if she even began that conversation. Most of them ended with him cutting things off between them in all ways he could.

Some ended worse.

And that was when a crazy, stupid, little idea struck her. Her dad had been dealing in demons since around the time he'd summoned Darr. In all those years, he may just have come across something useful. He wouldn't like the idea, but she was a grown woman. He no longer had the right to make her decisions for her, and she'd just have to make him see that. So she hurried to get dressed and darted to the nightstand for her cell phone.

It'd been a few months since she'd last talked to her father and, like always, her stomach knotted with the prospect of how this call would go. She loved him, and she could never cut him out of her life, but she honestly wished he'd change his ways. So much about his life disturbed her that she couldn't spend much time in his company anymore. Not even over the phone.

"Isolde? Is that you, baby?" He'd been answering her calls like that since she'd first moved out of the house in college.

"Yes, Dad," she replied obligingly. "How are you?" He'd expect the small talk, so she figured she'd do her best to just race through it.

Gerald sighed on the other end and she heard something *thump*, like a book or a heavy item hitting the floor. But his voice was calm when he spoke again. "Oh, I'm fine, sweetheart. Business is strong lately. I think I've even met a good woman. Maybe you'll let me introduce you to her if she sticks around for a few months?"

Izzy's heart clenched painfully in her chest. She hated when her father tried dating. As a teenager she'd been angry, thinking he was trying to replace her mother with some stranger. But as she'd grown she'd come to recognize that moving on didn't mean forgetting, and he wasn't. If there was one thing she knew about Gerald Duchane, it was that he'd never really be over his late wife. It was one of the few things they still had in common. "Maybe I will," she promised reluctantly. A few months could change everything, after all. "Listen, Dad, I'm sorry to cut the small talk, but I need to ask you about something. Do you have a minute?"

"For you, Izzy? Always."

Moving to sit on the edge of her bed and glancing nervously toward her closed door, she lowered her voice just a bit and chomped down on the proverbial bullet. "Is there a way to release Darr from the binding spell?"

Silence greeted her question. Seconds ticked by before her father finally asked, "Why would you want to know that? Aren't you two getting along?"

Fabulously. That's the problem. Releasing a breath, Izzy said, "Yes, it's just… This guilt eats me up, Dad." *There, truth.* "He's done so much for me. Besides, do you have *any* idea what it feels like to know that if you slip and break your neck an innocent person will die?"

Really, the Life Bond was a terrible curse. In the simplest terms if she died for *any* reason other than 'old age,' Darr would die, too. Whether he would suffer the same method of dying—or at least feel like he had—or his heart would just simply cease, neither of them knew. She'd asked on multiple occasions.

Her father spit out a bark of laughter. "Innocent? Izzy, sweetheart, I love that you have a good relationship with your bodyguard, but it's his job to protect you from things like slipping and breaking your neck. Besides, he's a demon. He's never been innocent. That's the beauty of it, honey. They're expendable."

Izzy's heart stalled in her chest and her breath caught in her throat. Had he really just said that? About *Darr*? About the *only* reason she was still breathing? About the man she loved? Tears of anger and irrational betrayal burning behind her eyes, Izzy snapped, "Then I must be expendable to you, too." She jabbed the End Call button and tossed the phone toward the far pillow, fighting back her sobs. *I can't believe he—*

"Izzy?" Darr was kneeling beside her, one warm hand on her thigh and worry in his eyes. He reached up with his other hand and brushed a wayward tear from her cheek with more tenderness than any *human* man had ever shown her. "What's wrong?"

Desperate to keep her composure, Izzy drew in a deep breath.

"That's the beauty of it, honey. They're expendable."

"That *bastard*!" she exclaimed furiously before she knew what she was doing. "How could he?"

Darr straightened and pulled her into his arms, taking a seat on her bed and allowing her to curl into him. With her head on his shoulder, his hand in her damp hair, and his cheek resting over her temple, he whispered soothing sounds in an effort to comfort her. "Shh. Take a deep breath, baby," he whispered. "I'm here. I'll help you through it."

Izzy's tears slowed as his words washed over her. In all their years together he'd never called her by any nickname other than the one she'd chosen for herself. But the tenderness in his words and actions now warmed her to her soul. Was there any way this man could possibly resent her for her father's choices?

Struggling to get a proper sentence out, Izzy said, "It-it's my father." She swallowed and let her eyes close. "He's a horrible man, isn't he?"

Darr was silent for several seconds, providing the answer she'd anticipated. Still, when he spoke, his voice was gentle. "He has redeeming qualities."

"Name one," Izzy challenged, looping her arms around his shoulders.

"He loves you." The response was immediate, leading her to believe this really was Darr's first answer. Perhaps his only. She certainly wouldn't blame him.

Even so, it wasn't enough for her in the moment. "Maybe," she allowed slowly, "but he does it wrong."

Again, Darr hesitated. "How so?"

Sniffling, Izzy mumbled, "He doesn't care about what I care about…" And that was far too close to a confession their newly-established relationship probably wasn't strong enough for just yet. Way, *way* too close.

Fortunately, before Darr could grill her on that slip-up, her cell began ringing again. It was her father's ringtone. Determined to ignore it, Izzy tightened her arms around him and did her best to bury her face in his shoulder. Damn did he smell good, too.

One of the arms around her waist pulled away, though, and the next thing she knew Darr was speaking. To her phone. "Mr. Duchane."

Izzy's throat went dry and she held her breath. What would her father say?

Apparently Darr had put her phone on speaker, because her father's vaguely distorted voice was louder than it should have been. "Hello, Darr. I'd like to speak to Izzy." There was no trace of the heartless bastard in his voice. It was sickening.

"She's here," Darr assured him. "You're on speaker."

"Oh," Gerald mumbled, a flicker of awkwardness passing through. He cleared his throat and added, "Izzy, sweetheart?"

Swallowing past her stubbornness, Izzy reluctantly lifted her head but made no move to reach for the phone. "My hanging up on you meant I don't want to talk anymore," she said. She needed to get him off the phone as quickly as possible, for so many reasons.

Gerald sighed heavily. "You take things too personally. I wasn't trying to be offensive, what I said was just the way the world works."

Renewed anger sparked inside her and Izzy loosened her hold on Darr in order to glare at the phone. "Well if that's how the world works then I'll go back to burying my head in the sand. Are you done?"

Darr raised a surprised brow at her, but remained silent. Respectful. She had half a mind to tell him what her father had said, but she worried he'd agree. Then she'd have to be mad at him, too.

"You're angry now, but you'll see," her father insisted. "In the meantime, I thought I'd answer your actual question. To apologize."

No! But she couldn't get her mouth to open. Her heart would rather hear the answer than avoid the argument.

"There is not a way to reverse a binding," her father said clearly. "I would remember if I'd come across one."

Her stomach sank like she'd swallowed a lead weight and her tears returned. Dropping her head back to Darr's shoulder she mumbled, "Hang up. Please."

"Izzy?"

"I'm sorry," Darr interrupted, "but Izzy's too upset to talk. Good day."

Silence reigned in the room after Darr disconnected the call. His arm came back around her supportively, but she could sense his building curiosity.

Of course he was going to ask. She would, if she were in his shoes. She just didn't know what she'd say.

After what seemed like an eternity, voice gentled again to respect her obvious mood, Darr broke the silence the only way he could.

"Why were you asking about breaking our bond?"

Chapter Seven

Izzy stiffened in his arms, but he wasn't surprised. Clearly she hadn't wanted him to know—at least not yet—that she was trying to break her father's binding spell. And despite the familiar guilt that flared in his chest at that enduring lie, Darr couldn't stop himself from worrying about what that desire could mean. Did she want to get away from him? Had he taken things too far?

The only way to know for certain was to pry it out of her, even if he had to ask repeatedly. It wasn't like he was going anywhere.

"It-it's not what it sounds like," Izzy finally whispered. She leaned back to look at him and he obligingly loosened his grip of her. He didn't dare yet release her entirely. At the brow he raised in response to her words, Izzy dropped her gaze. Her voice was nearly inaudible, even at this distance. "I don't want you to be stuck to me."

Stuck? So that was how she saw it.

Izzy took a breath and looked back up at him. Determination building in her brown eyes. "I love you, Darr. I don't want to be the face of some justifiable resentment or, worse, the ultimate death of you."

He reeled, nearly dropping her before he could gather himself. She *what*? "Shit."

Swallowing heavily, Izzy pressed on his chest until he released her and quickly backed a respectful distance away. She couldn't look at him. "I know that isn't what you wanted to hear. But it's the truth." Then she turned and practically ran from the room, leaving him alone.

Alone with his thoughts.

Alone with his frantic heart.

Alone with her lingering, mouthwatering scent.

Shit. Darr dragged a hand through his hair and stood, falling into a rapid pace. *She's in love with me.* How the hell had he managed that? And, more importantly, would she still when she learned he'd been lying all these years?

A growl ripped from him and he threw a fist into the nearest wall, needing to release at least a sliver of the confused energy swirling inside him. He needed to go find her, to finish this conversation. To tell her the truth. His lie no longer mattered. Not for anything other than to keep himself close to her.

Darr stopped, staring at but not really seeing her open bedroom door. He finally understood the real reason he hadn't opened up to her earlier. And as nice as that feeling was, it also brought with it a rather significant problem.

Shoving aside the prickle of fear tickling his heart, Darr strode from the room and skipped the stairs. She was probably in the kitchen, all the lights on so he couldn't sneak up on her, searching for something to turn into a muffin. That was what she did when she was flustered and didn't feel like she could talk it out.

The clatter of the muffin tin landing gracelessly on the stove top greeted his ears as he stepped out at the edge of the kitchen. Her back was to him and her counter was full of half the contents of the refrigerator. It was either going to be a mess of a muffin or she wasn't satisfied yet. He hoped there wouldn't wind up being any muffins at all.

"Izzy."

She stilled, though he knew she knew he was there. "It's okay," she finally said, stepping back with another handful of items balanced precariously over one arm. "I'm fine. You don't have to say anything."

"Lying's a sin you know," Darr teased as stepped into the kitchen.

Izzy scoffed and deposited her latest armload, closing the refrigerator door in the process. "It's one of those 'make it true' things. Takes time."

"Those do." He caught her wrist when she moved too close, stilling her movements and jarring her attention to him. "We should talk."

Her eyes shone with unshed tears and she pulled her arm from his loose grasp. "We really don't have to." She wasn't even trying to hide her fear. She opened her mouth to add more, but Darr moved first, catching her face between his palms and covering her lips with his. He needed her to listen and, most of all, he needed her to *not* cry.

Izzy melted into his mouth, her hands grabbing tight to his forearms with a moan.

He pulled back before he could forget himself. "Living room, please."

She nodded weakly and they moved to the sofa, her unpacked refrigerator ingredients forgotten. When they sat, Darr made sure to angle himself to face her, holding one of her hands in his.

"I screwed it all up, didn't I?" Her question was soft. Fragile.

He gave her hand a squeeze. "No, Izzy. But I may have."

Izzy frowned and looked up at him again. "But I'm the one who—"

"I've been lying to you." There was no delicate way to say it. Or, more accurately, he didn't know one. But his declaration did seem to catch her attention because her mouth snapped shut and her eyes went wide.

"You've...? About what?"

Darr pulled in a breath, doing his best to ignore the unfamiliar nerves twisting his stomach. Would that kiss he'd just stolen be their last? Should he wait another few decades before coming clean? *No.* He wasn't a coward and he couldn't do that to her, not knowing how she felt. "We're not bound."

Izzy reeled back, her hand jerking from his, and she exclaimed, "Don't be an ass, Darr. I'm capable of handling my own shit, okay?"

He couldn't quite stop the grin that twitched at his lips. "Careful, Izzy. Beautiful women shouldn't talk like demons even if they grew up with one."

Her eyes narrowed and he swore her hair got redder for an instant. "I'm serious! Just because you found out I want to set you free doesn't mean you can laugh at me!"

Swallowing the rest of his amusement, Darr slowly shook his head. "You misunderstand. You've already set me free, Izzy. In so many ways."

She slumped against the arm of the sofa and gave him a skeptical look. "I haven't been able to do anything."

"It started with your father," Darr explained. "He opened a portal into Hell right when I had finally escaped my master. But I was weak from a century of servitude and at a severe disadvantage, so I leapt into the portal and landed in your father's office."

Izzy's skepticism seemed to fade, falling away in favor of cautious curiosity. She said nothing as he spoke.

"It didn't take long to figure out he thought he'd summoned me specifically to protect you. Thought he'd placed me in a Life Bond. But in truth *all* he did was open a doorway for my escape."

She opened her mouth, stuttered something, and snapped it shut. With a shake of her head she finally said, "You're serious? But … then why stay?"

"Because a Life Bond was a perfect 'out'," Darr replied. He leaned forward and recaptured her hand in his. "Even if Creed found me, he couldn't take me back. I'd be useless to him. And Creed's not patient enough to wait an entire human lifespan. All I had to do was keep you alive for as long as possible."

Tears were shining in her eyes again. But so was hope. "So you don't hate me?" The question was fearful, hesitant, and heart-wrenching.

Darr growled and pulled her to him, kissing her thoroughly. He kept both hands tangled in her beautiful hair and devoured her lips. He sucked and stroked on her tongue, sweeping his tongue into her mouth in an erotic rhythm until Izzy was moaning and squirming against him. Until he could smell her desire wafting from her.

When he released her lips, allowing her to breathe, Darr rasped, "I'm sorry for lying to you, Izzy. I had no idea you were so upset about it." He paused so that she would feel the sincerity of his words before tilting her chin up to him again. With his nose brushing hers and her eyes locked onto his he added, "And I love you, too."
****

Izzy could barely breathe, her heart thrumming so loud in her chest Darr could've heard it even without his demonic hearing. None of that mattered. This whole situation was better than she could have—or ever had—dreamed. There was no bind. If she died, he didn't have to. That was almost better news than what he'd said next.

Her day would've been perfect if that was how it had ended.

After his quiet, thick confession, Izzy had launched herself at him. She'd managed to tackle him to the couch and she had every intention of pleasuring him until he couldn't tolerate it any longer.

That was when the most unexpected voice destroyed the moment.

"I knew it." The words were Zahk's, but his tone was different than what Izzy was used to. No levity, no smugness, no boredom. This tone was just *cold*.

"Zahk?" Darr questioned as he stood, facing his old friend and keeping Izzy half behind him.

Ice trickled down Izzy's spine and she swallowed her reflexive question. Something told her it really didn't matter why he'd neglected to knock on the front door. In fact, her instincts were screaming that his presence was bad. Very, very bad. "Darr…"

"Looks like your lover's catching on, D," Zahk said in that same cold voice. It was all wrong for his words.

"What are you doing here, Zahk? You know you can't just pop in." His words were typical, but Izzy heard the hesitation in his voice. He'd noticed something off, too.

Something flickered in Zahk's eyes, something like emotion, but it was gone just as fast. "I'd ask you to forgive me," he started as another shadow swirled beside him. "But you won't be alive to do it." Jerking his chin toward Izzy, Zahk added, "Neither will your bitch."

The shadows solidified and settled, revealing Creed in all his nightmarish glory. In better lighting Izzy could finally see that Creed was clearly a demon who reveled in his power. He even had pointy teeth and glowing, red eyes over pale, almost gray, skin. It was no wonder he stuck to the shadows.

"Good evening, Darr," Creed greeted with a sickly smile. "It's good news that you're not really bound. That means she doesn't have to die *first*."

Izzy swallowed and Darr stepped fully in front of her. "You betrayed me," he said. She couldn't see his face, but she was sure the words were for Zahk. And if she felt sick to her stomach over this turn of events she could only imagine how hard it was on Darr.

"No," Zahk replied. "I was never with you."

"I don't suppose you'll surrender?" Creed offered. Izzy caught a glimpse of an extended arm and figured he was gesturing largely. At Darr's silence he added darkly, "If, perhaps, only for her survival?"

Cold dread shot through her so fast Izzy didn't realize she'd found her feet. "Not a chance!"

Darr's hand landed on her shoulder, holding her back before she could do anything dumb. Or, well, dumber. Still, when Darr spoke, his words weren't for her. "You heard the lady."

All hell broke loose after that.

Creed and Zahk lunged in sync and the air in the room thickened so badly Izzy could hardly breathe. A dark energy blast erupted in the middle of the room, two on one, and Izzy went flying backward. She heard Darr grunt from what sounded like a heavy impact only moments before she herself crashed into a sturdy wall. Pain exploded in a blinding flash behind her eyes and she sagged to the ground, barely aware.

Something that sounded like an angry roar filled the air, reverberating in her ears, but Izzy could only barely keep her eyes open. Figures were blurry and she had a building coppery taste in her mouth. *Like blood...*

Suddenly blackness swallowed what little vision she had, but her limited awareness remained and she knew she wasn't unconscious. Even when she registered arms around her and solid ground under her feet, the blackness was slow to recede. And she could hear something. It sounded insistent, but she couldn't quite make it out.

Familiar ashen eyes drew her attention. Ashen eyes above a taut mouth and a strong, stubbly jaw. *Darr…?*

Images of Zahk popped up, scattered, in her mind's eye. Seeing him at the lake with Darr. Meeting him as a teenager. Freaking out the first time he appeared in her house unannounced. His refusal to help Darr in the last confrontation with Creed. *Traitor.*

"—un!" It sounded like Darr, but she still wasn't sure what he was saying.

She groaned his name, trying to fight past her raging headache and concentrate. Darr's voice sounded urgent. Urgent like she'd never known.

"—mit, Izzy, *run!*" He finished the command with an inelegant shove, trying to jump-start her run even as he turned and sprinted off after another demon. Creed.

He was still fighting Zahk and Creed. All on his own. And he expected her to run?

Pushing herself up on her wobbly legs, Izzy hesitated. She already had what she assumed was a serious head injury given her present state. What good would she really be in a fight against two demons? *None.* She would only be in the way. A liability.

"If I ever tell you to run," Darr said seriously, *crouched before her to look her in the eyes. She loved his eyes. They were strong and honest; reliable. Like him. "Then run. Run as fast as you can until you can get somewhere safe. Find help if you're able."*

The memory faded on that last word, but Izzy had heard enough. He'd given her that instruction when she was but fourteen years old. Apparently it was still a good lesson to keep in mind. So she turned and ran deep into the forested area behind her house, ever grateful for having chosen to live on the outskirts of town.

She ran until she could only barely hear the reverberating explosions. And then it was time to get help. She could only think of one kind of help worth searching for and, as odd as it felt, she figured if it was going to work she'd need to give it her all.

Izzy hit her knees, clasped her hands, and closed her eyes in prayer. Not that she'd seen a single day in church since her mother's funeral. But all she had to do was think, right? *"Please, if you're out there... Kai, I need your help. Darr needs your help. You said you wanted Creed. I know where he is."*

She had just long enough to think that she really hoped she hadn't just made a huge mistake when the wind shifted.

"Praying, are we?"

Izzy's mouth went dry. That wasn't the voice of the angel she'd briefly met.

****

Darr wiped a trail of blood from his lips and kept his eye on his enemy. Zahk had fled around the time he'd told Izzy to run. Leaving just him and Creed. His former master. The face—the voice—of most of his nightmares. The problem with Creed wasn't his fondness for slaves. It was his power. Creed was rumored to share the blood of an old and powerful demon, one of Satan's closest subordinates. Which meant he had power and poison to spare.

"What's the matter, slave?" Creed taunted with a battle crazed smirk. "Give up so soon?"

"Never," Darr swore, shoving to his feet. Creed had him outclassed, but the bastard didn't have his motivation. If Darr fell there would be no one to protect Izzy.

Creed sprang forward without warning, curving a veritable blade of dark energy around his hand and releasing it with a vicious swing of his arm. Darr rolled and let his shoulder slam into the bottom edge, grinding his teeth against the pain as the rest of the attack shattered.

The beautiful thing about dark energy was that any demon could use it. There was no 'specific flavor' attuned to one demon or one bloodline. So when Creed's homemade weapon shattered, Darr was in the perfect position to gather the pieces and mold them into something new. It took only a tiny bit of his own energy to fashion the sphere and even less to hurl it straight at Creed's rotten head.

He didn't expect it to work, but he hoped it would be a good distraction. If he was really lucky, it'd even slow him down.

****

"Zahk." Somehow, Izzy was less than surprised to see that she'd been followed. "You son of a bitch." She wanted to gouge his eyes out for betraying Darr like he had.

Zahk's lips twitched. "Right back at you, whore," he returned. "I always knew that story about the bond was bullshit."

"Would that really have held you back?" Because frankly, she doubted it. A lot.

Zahk shrugged and stepped closer. "Not my call. And Creed's a little busy killing your toy."

"He'll fail," Izzy snapped. "Darr's strong. He'll survive."

"Hmm." Zahk crowded her against a tall tree trunk. Leaning in close he whispered, "And do you think that'll be enough for him? Once you're dead, I mean?"

Izzy swallowed heavily.

"I for one would kind of like to see," Zahk continued, reaching out and playing with her hair. "Any last requests?"

Izzy thought about spitting in his face, or seeing if she could land a knee in his undoubtedly tiny balls, but before she could more than begin to decide the decision was taken from her.

"Demon." The voice was harsh and threatening. Full of power.

Kai.

Zahk turned his gaze reflexively, his eyes bulging when he realized who had called to him. He released her and landed a foot in the tree's shadow, but it was too late. Kai was standing too close to miss when he drew his sword. Zahk screamed, the sound wet and sickening, before disappearing forever in a burst of black demonic flame. Leaving behind nothing but an unusually blue scorch.

Kai turned to Izzy, flickering sword at his side, and wasted no time getting to the punch line. "Where is Creed?"

****

Darr bit back an outcry of pain as Creed's newly acquired spear of splintered wood impaled him. It had missed his heart, and probably his lungs, but not by much. Instead of lingering on the pain, Darr grabbed hold of the spear and jerked it straight back. He managed to tear a good chunk out of Creed's arm.

Creed laughed loudly. "That may be the best hit you've ever landed on me!" He glanced toward his bleeding, gouged arm with a sick grin. "I might be impressed. It's a shame you don't see the value in torture."

"One of the many things we'll never agree on," Darr returned tightly. His chest hurt like hell and though he'd survive, he was going to be weaker than he'd been in decades. For a while, at least—and that was assuming he lived through the fight.

"That has to hurt," Creed said, mock-cringing as he studied the wound he'd inflicted. Then he lifted his stare to Darr and his lips twitched. "Let's see how much more I can hurt you."

Darr braced himself, debating the wisdom of drawing on more dark energy to fight with over reserving his power. He almost didn't notice Creed freeze. But freeze he had, right in his tracks. Creed's expression curved into an angry snarl and he straightened. *What caught his attention?*

An image of Izzy immediately filled his mind and Darr realized Creed was now staring in the direction she'd fled. He reacted on instinct.

With a roar Darr launched and tackled Creed to the ground. They tore into the topsoil with their impact, dragging back several feet, each struggling to get the upper hand. Until Creed threw his weight into nearly knocking Darr off balance and Darr's shoulder slammed into a tree.

"Thanks," Creed said a moment before disappearing into the shadows around them.

Darr barely had a moment to process what had happened before the reason why made itself known.

"You let him escape." It wasn't a question. And it wasn't Izzy.

Darr looked over, landing on one knee, and realized that itch to run had been because there was a damned angel walking up. The same so-called warrior angel who'd bailed them out of the problem at the resort, supposedly in the name of chasing Creed. This time he wore battle leathers and wielded a sword at his side—a sword surrounded by flickering white-blue flame.

"Darr!" *That* was Izzy. She bolted from behind the angel, running to him and dropping to her knees at his side. "You're hurt!"

Ignoring the angel for a moment, Darr dragged his gaze up and down Izzy's figure. She had some scrapes, but aside from her head injury there was nothing too bad. Nothing an unplanned flight through brush couldn't be to blame for. "Are you all right?"

Izzy frowned and tears pooled in her shining eyes. "I won't be if you die, you idiot." There was no venom in her voice. Just unsteady wavering and concern.

"Demon."

Knowing it wasn't smart, especially in his weakened condition, to continue ignoring the angel, Darr looked back to him. Kai hadn't moved a step. He still held his sword, at his side in a semi-relaxed state that instinct insisted was an illusion. Just one glance into this being's eyes was enough to assure *anyone* that he was not to be fucked with. "Why are you here?" Shouldn't he have gone after Creed?

Kai's eyes narrowed almost imperceptibly. "Isolde prayed for assistance. She offered Creed in return. Why did you let him escape?"

"I said I knew where he was," Izzy interrupted. But her voice betrayed her. She recognized the danger in this situation, too.

"It isn't like I was *trying* to," Darr reminded. "He had the upper hand." *Again.* And while that didn't surprise him, it did infuriate him. Creed was older, from a stronger line, and had fought his way to a position of power in Hell. It was natural that Darr wouldn't stack up to him, but damn if that didn't do a thing to make him feel better. Instead of dwelling on that, though, Darr refocused on the current problem. It wasn't nearly out of the question that this angel wouldn't decide to kill him.

And what would happen to Izzy if he died?

Chapter Eight

Izzy held her breath as Kai studied Darr. In the moment praying for help had seemed like such a good idea, but now … now she was terrified that she would be responsible for the death of the person she loved most in all the world. Such a tragedy would kill her. She wanted to fall to her knees between them and plead for Darr's life, but she didn't dare. Darr would be insulted and this angel didn't seem like the kind of man who had much tolerance for—well, anything.

Has it really come down to this?

When she was a child, believing herself newly bound to a dark and powerful demon, Izzy had envisioned herself untouchable. Finally free. Even when her father's work and increasingly questionable methods endangered her life she had never really been scared. Never felt held back or infringed upon. Because Darr was with her. This man with more power than she knew how to describe and just enough control to pass for human when necessary. As her father pulled away, Darr became her everything. Her rock, her savior. She fell in love with him like it was inevitable, and when he'd finally touched her … the best way to describe how she felt was 'pure bliss.'

How could something so right, so perfect, so *destined*, be cut down now? When it had barely gotten off the ground? How would she survive losing him?

She'd nearly forgotten herself when Kai finally spoke again.

"It is against my nature to let a demon survive in this realm." Flicking his blue gaze between them, he added pointedly, "Twice."

Darr grunted under his breath and pushed to his feet. He was moving slower than usual. *Of course he is. He has a giant hole in his chest.* He made no move to step forward. He held his ground at her side, fists unclenched. Facing his fate head on.

Izzy's heart clenched and she could barely draw a breath around the lump in her throat. There was no stopping the tears, so she focused on holding back the sobs.

"But I feel inclined to make an exception in your case," Kai declared, his tone detached. He narrowed his eyes on Darr and added, "Make no mistake. Your service in protecting this innocent heart is what has earned your freedom. Betray her, corrupt her beyond salvation, or become more of a danger than a savior, and I will make you cease to exist."

"What…?" The breathless question was past Izzy's lips before she could think better of it.

Kai looked back to her calmly. "You prayed for assistance."

A smile threatened to tip her lips as more tears spilled over. If she'd been strong enough to stand, she might have run to hug him without a thought. "Thank you."

Kai tucked his sword into the slim sheath on his waist with a faint nod. A moment later bright wings sprouted from his back and stretched wide. Each white feather was outlined by a thin, beautiful layer of nearly-white blue flame. Like some kind of holy fire. A single flap of those massive wings shot him skyward with all the force of a rocket. And then he was gone.

Izzy released an audible gasp of breath and slumped. *He didn't die.* She hadn't gotten her lover killed. In her peripheral vision she saw Darr reach up, toward his chest, and finally remembered his wound. It was bad.

Only, when she turned to look at it, he was prodding solid flesh.

"Darr…?"

He lifted a smile to her and knelt in front of her. "Healed by an angel. Who'd have guessed?"

Hours later they lay in Izzy's large bed, Darr's arm curled around her torso tightly. Her ear pressed over his heart, listening to the steady rhythm it had fallen into, she whispered, "I'm so glad you survived…"

Darr pressed his lips to her hair. "I won't leave you that easily."

Izzy smiled and pressed her fingertips into his chest. "I don't want you to leave me ever." Even though he surely would. What sort of self-respecting immortal kept an old, wrinkly, maybe wheelchair-bound lover? And someday that would be her. Hell, her grandmother had had Alzheimer's, so there was always the chance she would, too. Or one of any number of other things. So she just had to make the best of this time while she had it.

"Izzy," Darr began, his quiet voice almost urgent. "There's something I want to ask you."

Pushing back her depressing thoughts, Izzy lifted her head enough to find his eyes. He'd made no move to release her so she stayed as she was. "What is it?"

"There are … other types of life binding spells," he finally said. It was obvious he was choosing his words carefully so she stayed silent. Waiting. "There are one or two which unite two souls for all time. They do mean dying together, yes, but that doesn't have to be a bad thing."

Izzy frowned. "How couldn't it be?"

His hand came up, thumb landing along her lower lip tenderly. "I don't *want* to outlive you, Isolde Duchane. I would rather bind our souls so tightly that we can never be torn apart."

Her heart rammed against her ribcage as she began to suspect his angle. His *glorious* angle. "Darr…"

"The choice is yours completely." He paused, swallowed audibly, and added, "You could refuse outright, of course. Or you can choose one of two varieties. We can tie our lives to your lifespan … or to mine."

Izzy blinked. "But … wouldn't I still age?"

Darr shook his head. "Not a day."

Then it was no contest. She knew exactly what she wanted.

With a smile splitting her face and a tear slipping free, Izzy pressed her lips to his and murmured, "Let's live forever, lover."

The End

www.rosewulf.weebly.com

Evernight Publishing

www.evernightpublishing.com